Edgar Wallace was born illegitimately adopted by George Freeman, a porter at eleven, Wallace sold newspapers at Ludg. school took a job with a printer. He enlist ,... west Kent Regiment, later transferring to the Medical Staff Corps and was sent to South Africa. In 1898 he published a collection of poems called *The Mission that Failed*, left the army and became a correspondent for Reuters.

Wallace became the South African war correspondent for *The Daily Mail*. His articles were later published as *Unofficial Dispatches* and his outspokenness infuriated Kitchener, who banned him as a war correspondent until the First World War. He edited the *Rand Daily Mail*, but gambled disastrously on the South African Stock Market, returning to England to report on crimes and hanging trials. He became editor of *The Evening News*, then in 1905 founded the Tallis Press, publishing *Smith*, a collection of soldier stories, and *Four Just Men*. At various times he worked on *The Standard*, *The Star*, *The Week-End Racing Supplement* and *The Story Journal*.

In 1917 he became a Special Constable at Lincoln's Inn and also a special interrogator for the War Office. His first marriage to Ivy Caldecott, daughter of a missionary, had ended in divorce and he married his much younger secretary, Violet King.

The Daily Mail sent Wallace to investigate atrocities in the Belgian Congo, a trip that provided material for his *Sanders of the River* books. In 1923 he became Chairman of the Press Club and in 1931 stood as a Liberal candidate at Blackpool. On being offered a scriptwriting contract at RKO, Wallace went to Hollywood. He died in 1932, on his way to work on the screenplay for *King Kong*.

The Avenger

HOUSE OF
STRATUS

This edition published in 2001 by House of Stratus, an imprint of Stratus Holdings plc, 24c Old Burlington Street, London, W1X 1RL, UK.

www.houseofstratus.com

Typeset, printed and bound by House of Stratus.

A catalogue record for this book is available from the British Library.

ISBN 1-84232-659-7

We would like to thank the Edgar Wallace Society for all the support they have given House of Stratus. Enquiries on how to join the Edgar Wallace Society should be addressed to: The Edgar Wallace Society, c/o Penny Wyrd, 84 Ridgefield Road, Oxford, OX4 3DA. Email: info@edgarwallace.org Web: http://www.edgarwallace.org/

CONTENTS

THE HEAD-HUNTER

Captain Mike Brixan had certain mild and innocent superstitions. He believed, for example, that if he saw a green crow in a field he would certainly see another green crow before the day was out. And when, at the bookstand on Aix la Chapelle station, he saw and purchased a dime novel that was comprehensively intituled "Only an Extra, or the Pride of Hollywood," he was less concerned as to how this thrilling and dog-eared romance came to be on offer at half a million marks (this was in the days when marks were worth money) than as to the circumstances in which he would again hear or read the word "extras" in the sense of a supernumerary and unimportant screen actress.

The novel did not interest him at all. He read one page of superlatives and turned for relief to the study of a Belgian timetable. He was bored, but not so bored that he could interest himself in the sensational rise of the fictitious Rosa Love from modest obscurity to a press agent and wealth.

But "extra" was a new one on Michael, and he waited for the day to bring its inevitable companion.

To say that he was uninterested in crime, that burglars were less thrilling than golf scores, and the record of murders hardly worth the reading, might convey a wrong impression to those who knew him as the cleverest agent in the Foreign Office Intelligence Department.

His official life was spent in meeting queer continentals in obscure restaurants and, in divers rôles, to learn of the undercurrents that were drifting the barques of diplomacy to unsuspected ports. He had twice roamed through Europe in the guise of an open-mouthed tourist; had canoed many hundred miles through the gorges of the Danube to discover, in little riverside beer-houses, the inward meanings of secret mobilizations. These were tasks wholly to his liking.

Therefore he was not unnaturally annoyed when he was withdrawn from Berlin at a moment when, as it seemed, the mystery of the Slovak Treaty was in a way to being solved, for he had secured, at a cost, a rough but accurate draft.

"I should have had a photograph of the actual document if you had left me another twenty-four hours," he reproached his chief, Major George Staines, when he reported himself at Whitehall next morning.

"Sorry," replied that unrepentant man, "but the truth is, we've had a heart to heart talk with the Slovakian Prime Minister, and he has promised to behave and practically given us the text of the treaty – it was only a commercial affair. Mike, did you know Elmer?"

The Foreign Office detective sat down on the edge of the table.

"Have you brought me from Berlin to ask me that?" he demanded bitterly. "Have you taken me from my favourite café, on Unter den Linden – by the way, the Germans are making small arm ammunition by the million at a converted pencil factory in Bavaria – to discuss Elmer? He's a clerk, isn't he?"

Major Staines nodded.

"He *was*," he said, "in the Accountancy Department. He disappeared from view three weeks ago, and an examination of his books showed that he had been systematically stealing funds which were under his control."

Mike Brixan made a little face.

"I'm sorry to hear that," he said. "He seemed to be a fairly quiet and inoffensive man. But surely you don't want me to go after him? That is a job for Scotland Yard."

"I don't want you to go after him," said Staines slowly, "because – well, he has been found."

There was something very significant and sinister in his tone, and before he could take the little slip of paper from the portfolio on the desk, Michael Brixan knew what was coming.

"Not the Head-Hunter?" he gasped. Even Michael knew about the Head-Hunter.

Staines nodded.

"Here's the note."

He handed the typewritten slip across to his subordinate, and Michael read:

You will find a box in the hedge by the railway arch at Esher.
                                                    THE HEAD-HUNTER

"The Head-Hunter!" repeated Michael mechanically, and whistled.

"We found the box, and of course we found the unfortunate Elmer's head, sliced neatly from his body," said Staines. "This is the twelfth head in seven years," Staines went on, "and in almost every case – in fact, in every case except two – the victim has been a fugitive from justice. Even if the treaty question had not been settled, Mike, I should have brought you back."

"But this is a police job," said the young man, troubled.

"Technically you're a policeman," interrupted his chief, "and the Foreign Secretary wishes you to take this case in hand, and he does this with the full approval of the Secretary of State, who of course controls Scotland Yard. So far, the death of Francis Elmer and the discovery of his gruesome remains have not been given out to the press. There was such a fuss last time that the police want to keep this quiet. They have had an inquest – I guess the jury was picked, but it would be high treason to say so – and the usual verdict has been returned. The only information I can give you is that Elmer was seen by his niece a week ago in Chichester. We discovered this before the man's fate was known. The girl, Adele Leamington, is working for the Knebworth Film Corporation, which has its studio in Chichester. Old Knebworth is an American and a very good sort. The girl is a sort of super-chorus extra, that's the word – "

Michael gasped.

"Extra! I knew that infernal word would turn up again. Go on, sir – what do you wish me to do?"

"Go along and see her," said the chief. "Here is the address."

"Is there a Mrs Elmer?" asked Michael as he put the slip into his pocket.

The other nodded.

"Yes, but she can throw no light upon the murder. She, by the way, is the only person who knows he is dead. She had not seen her husband for a month, and apparently they had been more or less separated for years. She benefits considerably by his death, for he was well insured in her favour."

Michael read again the gruesome note from the Head-Hunter.

"What is your theory about this?" he asked curiously.

"The general idea is that he is a lunatic who feels called upon to mete out punishment to defaulters. But the two exceptions disturb that theory pretty considerably."

Staines lay back in his chair, a puzzled frown on his face.

"Take the case of Willitt. His head was found on Clapham Common two years ago. Willitt was a well-off man, the soul of honesty, well liked, and he had a very big balance at his bank. Crewling, the second exception, who was one of the first of the Hunter's victims, was also above suspicion, though in his case there is no doubt he was mentally unbalanced a few weeks before his death.

"The typewritten notification has invariably been typed out on the same machine. In every case you have the half-obliterated 'u', the faint 'g', and the extraordinary alignment which the experts are unanimous in ascribing to a very old and out-of-date Kost machine. Find the man who uses that typewriter and you have probably found the murderer. But it is very unlikely that he will ever be found that way, for the police have published photographs pointing out the peculiarities of type, and I should imagine that Mr Hunter does not use this machine except to announce the demise of his victims."

Michael Brixan went back to his flat, a little more puzzled and a little more worried by his unusual commission. He moved and had his being in the world of high politics. The finesses of diplomacy were his peculiar study, and the normal abnormalities of humanity, the thefts and murders and larcenies which occupied the attention of the constabulary, did not come into his purview.

"Bill," said he, addressing the small terrier that lay on the hearth-rug before the fireless grate of his sitting-room, "this is where I fall down. But whether I do or not, I'm going to meet an extra – ain't that grand?"

Bill wagged his tail agreeably.

MR SAMPSON LONGVALE CALLS

Adele Leamington waited till the studio was almost empty before she came to where the white-haired man sat crouched in his canvas chair, his hands thrust into his trousers pockets, a malignant scowl on his forehead.

It was not a propitious moment to approach him: nobody knew that better than she.

"Mr Knebworth, may I speak to you?"

He looked up slowly. Ordinarily he would have risen, for this middle-aged American in normal moments was the soul of courtesy. But just at that moment, his respect for womanhood was something below zero. His look was blank, though the director in him instinctively approved her values. She was pretty, with regular features, a mop of brown hair in which the sunshine of childhood still lingered. Her mouth firm, delicately shaped, her figure slim – perfect in many ways.

Jack had seen many beautiful extras in his career, and had passed through stages of enthusiasm and despair as he had seen them translated to the screen – pretty wooden figures without soul or expression, gauche of movement, hopeless. Too pretty to be clever, too conscious of their beauty to be natural. Dolls without intelligence or initiative – just "extras" who could wear clothes in a crowd, who could smile and dance mechanically, fit for extras and nothing else all the days of their lives.

"Well?" he asked brusquely.

"Is there a part I could play in this production, Mr Knebworth?" she asked.

His shaven lips curled.

"Aren't you playing a part, Miss — can't remember your name — Leamington, is it?"

"I'm certainly playing – I'm one of the figures in the background," she smiled. "I don't want a big part, but I'm sure I could do better than I have done."

"I'm mighty sure you couldn't do worse than some people," he growled. "No, there's no part for you, friend. There'll be no story to shoot unless things alter. That's what!"

She was going away when he recalled her.

"Left a good home, I guess?" he said. "Thought picture-making meant a million dollars a year an' a new automobile every Thursday? Or maybe you were holding down a good job as a stenographer and got it under your toque that you'd make Hollywood feel small if you got your chance? Go back home, kid, and tell the old man that a typewriter's got a sunlight arc beaten to death as an instrument of commerce."

The girl smiled faintly.

"I didn't come into pictures because I was stage-struck, if that is what you mean, Mr Knebworth. I came in knowing just how hard a life it might be. I have no parents."

He looked up at her curiously.

"How do you live?" he asked. "There's no money in 'extra' work – not on this lot, anyway. Might be if I was one of those billion dollar directors who did pictures with chariot races. But I don't. My ideal picture has got five characters."

"I have a little income from my mother, and I write," said the girl.

She stopped as she saw him looking past her to the studio entrance, and, turning her head, saw a remarkable figure standing in the doorway. At first she thought it was an actor who had made up for a film test.

The newcomer was an old man, but his great height and erect carriage would not have conveyed that impression at a distance. The tight-fitting tail-coat, the trousers strapped to his boots, the high collar and black satin stock belonged to a past age, though they were newly made. The white linen bands that showed at his wrists were goffered, his double-breasted waistcoat of grey velvet was fastened by golden buttons. He might have stepped from a family portrait of one of those dandies of the 'fifties. He held a tall hat in one gloved hand, a hat with a curly brim, and in the other a gold-topped walking-stick. The face, deeply lined, was benevolent and kind, and he seemed unconscious of his complete baldness.

Jack Knebworth was out of his chair in a second and walked toward the stranger.

"Why, Mr Longvale, I am glad to see you – did you get my letter? I can't tell you how much obliged I am to you for the loan of your house."

Sampson Longvale, of the Dower House! She remembered now. He was known in Chichester as "the old-fashioned gentleman," and once, when she was out on location, somebody had pointed out the big, rambling house, with its weed-grown garden and crumbling walls, where he lived.

"I thought I would come over and see you," said the big man.

His voice was rich and beautifully modulated. She did not remember having heard a voice quite as sweet, and she looked at the eccentric figure with a new interest.

"I can only hope that the house and grounds are suitable to your requirements. I am afraid they are in sad disorder, but I cannot afford to keep the estate in the same condition as my grandfather did."

"Just what I want, Mr Longvale. I was afraid you might be offended when I told you – "

The old gentleman interrupted him with a soft laugh.

"No, no, I wasn't offended, I was amused. You needed a haunted house: I could even supply that quality, though I will not promise you that my family ghost will walk. The Dower House has been haunted for hundreds of years. A former occupant in a fit of frenzy murdered his daughter there, and the unhappy lady is supposed to walk. I have never seen her, though many years ago one of my servants did. Fortunately, I am relieved of that form of annoyance: I no longer keep servants in the house," he smiled, "though, if you care to stay the night, I shall be honoured to entertain five or six of your company."

Knebworth heaved a sigh of relief. He had made diligent inquiries and found that it was almost impossible to secure lodgings in the neighbourhood, and he was most anxious to take night pictures, and for one scene he particularly desired the peculiar light value which he could only obtain in the early hours of the morning.

"I'm afraid that would give you a lot of trouble, Mr Longvale," he said. "And here and now I think we might discuss that delicate subject of—"

The old man stopped him with a gesture.

"If you are going to speak of money, please don't," he said firmly. "I am interested in cinematography; in fact, I am interested in most modern things. We old men are usually prone to decry modernity, but I find my chiefest pleasure in the study of those scientific wonders which this new age has revealed to us."

He looked at the director quizzically.

"Some day you shall take a picture of me in the one rôle in which I think I should have no peer — a picture of me in the role of my illustrious ancestor."

Jack Knebworth stared, half amused, half startled. It was no unusual experience to find people who wished to see themselves on the screen, but he never expected that little piece of vanity from Mr Sampson Longvale.

"I should be glad," he said formally. "Your people were pretty well known, I guess?"

Mr Longvale sighed.

"It is my regret that I do not come from the direct line that included Charles Henry, the most historic member of my family. He was my great-uncle. I come from the Bordeaux branch of Longvales, which has made history, sir." He shook his head regretfully.

"Are you French, Mr Longvale?" asked Jack.

Apparently the old man did not hear him. He was staring into space. Then, with a start: "Yes, yes, we were French. My great grandfather married an English lady whom he met in peculiar circumstances. We came to England in the days of the directorate."

Then, for the first time, he seemed aware of Adele's presence, and bowed toward her.

"I think I must go," he said, taking a huge gold watch from his fob pocket.

The girl watched them as they passed out of the hall, and presently she saw the "old-fashioned gentleman" pass the window, driving the oldest-fashioned car she had ever seen. It must have been one of the first motorcars ever introduced into the country, a great, upstanding, cumbersome machine, that passed with a thunderous sound and at no great speed down the gravel drive out of sight.

Presently Jack Knebworth came slowly back.

"This craze for being screened certainly gets 'em – old or young," he said. "Good night, Miss – forget your name – Leamington, ain't it? Good night."

She was halfway home before she realized that the conversation that she had plucked up such courage to initiate had ended unsatisfactorily for her, and she was as far away from her small part as ever.

THE NIECE

Adele Leamington occupied a small room in a small house, and there were moments when she wished it were smaller, that she might be justified in plucking up her courage to ask from the stout and unbending Mrs Watson, her landlady, a reduction of rent. The extras on Jack Knebworth's lot were well paid but infrequently employed; for Jack was one of those clever directors who specialized in domestic stories.

She was dressing when Mrs Watson brought in her morning cup of tea.

"There's a young fellow been hanging round outside since I got up," said Mrs Watson. "I saw him when I took in the milk. Very polite he was, but I told him you weren't awake."

"Did he want to see me?" asked the astonished girl.

"That's what he said," said Mrs Watson grimly. "I asked him if he came from Knebworth, and he said no. If you want to see him, you can have the use of the parlour, though I don't like young men calling on young girls. I've never let theatrical lodgings before, and you can't be too careful. I've always had a name for respectability and I want to keep it."

Adele smiled.

"I cannot imagine anything more respectable than an early morning caller, Mrs Watson," she said.

She went downstairs and opened the door. The young man was standing on the sidewalk with his back to her, but at the sound of the door opening he turned. He was good-looking and well-dressed, and his smile was quick and appealing.

"I hope your landlady did not bother to wake you up? I could have waited. You are Miss Adele Leamington, aren't you?"

She nodded.

"Will you come in, please?" she asked, and took him into the stuffy little front parlour, and, closing the door behind her, waited.

"I am a reporter," he said untruthfully, and her face fell.

"You've come about Uncle Francis? Is anything really wrong? They sent a detective to see me a week ago. Have they found him?"

"No, they haven't found him," he said carefully. "You knew him very well, of course, Miss Leamington?"

She shook her head.

"No, I have only seen him twice in my life. My dear father and he quarrelled before I was born, and I only saw him once after daddy died, and once before mother was taken with her fatal illness."

She heard him sigh, and sensed his relief, though why he should be relieved that her uncle was almost a stranger to her, she could not fathom.

"You saw him at Chichester, though?" he said.

She nodded.

"Yes, I saw him. I was on my way to Goodwood Park – a whole party of us in a char-à-banc – and I saw him for a moment walking along the side-walk. He looked desperately ill and worried. He was just coming out of a stationer's shop when I saw him; he had a newspaper under his arm and a letter in his hand."

"Where was the store?" he asked quickly.

She gave him the address, and he jotted it down.

"You didn't see him again?"

She shook her head.

"Is anything really very badly wrong?" she asked anxiously. "I've often heard mother say that Uncle Francis was very extravagant, and a little unscrupulous. Has he been in trouble?"

"Yes," admitted Michael, "he has been in trouble, but nothing that you need worry about. You're a great film actress, aren't you?"

In spite of her anxiety she laughed.

"The only chance I have of being a great film actress is for you to say so in your paper."

"My what?" he asked, momentarily puzzled. "Oh yes, my newspaper, of course!"

"I don't believe you're a reporter at all," she said with sudden suspicion.

"Indeed I am," he said glibly, and dared to pronounce the name of that widely-circulated sheet upon which the sun seldom sets.

"Though I'm not a great actress, and fear I never shall be, I like to believe it is because I've never had a chance – I've a horrible suspicion that Mr Knebworth knows instinctively that I am no good."

Mike Brixan had found a new interest in the case, an interest which, he was honest enough to confess to himself, was not dissociated from the niece of Francis Elmer. He had never met anybody quite so pretty and quite so unsophisticated and natural.

"You're going to the studio, I suppose?"

She nodded.

"I wonder if Mr Knebworth would mind my calling to see you?"

She hesitated.

"Mr Knebworth doesn't like callers."

"Then maybe I'll call on him," said Michael, nodding. "It doesn't matter whom I call on, does it?"

"It certainly doesn't matter to me," said the girl coldly.

"In the vulgar language of the masses," thought Mike as he strode down the street, "I have had the bird!"

His inquiries did not occupy very much of his time. He found the little news shop, and the proprietor, by good fortune, remembered the coming of Mr Francis Elmer.

"He came for a letter, though it wasn't addressed to Elmer," said the shopkeeper. "A lot of people have their letters addressed here. I make a little extra money that way."

"Did he buy a newspaper?"

"No, sir, he did not buy a newspaper; he had one under his arm – the *Morning Telegram*. I remember that, because I noticed that he'd put a blue pencil mark round one of the agony advertisements on the front page, and I was wondering what it was all about. I kept a copy of that day's *Morning Telegram*: I've got it now."

He went into the little parlour at the back of the shop and returned with a dingy newspaper, which he laid on the counter.

"There are six there, but I don't know which one it was."

Michael examined the agony advertisements. There was one frantic message from a mother to her son, asking him to return and saying that "all would be forgiven." There was a cryptogram message, which he had not time to decipher. A third, which was obviously the notice of an assignation. The fourth was a thinly veiled advertisement for a new hairwaver, and at the fifth he stopped. It ran:

Troubled. Final directions at address I gave you. Courage. Benefactor.

"Some 'benefactor,'" said Mike Brixan. "What was he like – the man who called? Was he worried?"

"Yes, sir: he looked upset – all distracted like. He seemed like a chap who'd lost his head."

"That seems a fair description," said Mike.

THE LEADING LADY

In the studio of the Knebworth Picture Corporation the company had been waiting in its street clothes for the greater part of an hour.

Jack Knebworth sat in his conventional attitude, huddled up in his canvas chair, fingering his long chin and glaring from time to time at the clock above the studio manager's office.

It was eleven when Stella Mendoza flounced in, bringing with her the fragrance of wood violets and a small, unhappy Peke.

"Do you work to summer-time?" asked Knebworth slowly. "Or maybe you thought the call was for afternoon? You've kept fifty people waiting, Stella."

"I can't help their troubles," she said with a shrug of shoulder. "You told me you were going on location, and naturally I didn't expect there would be any hurry. I had to pack my things."

"Naturally you didn't think there was any hurry!"

Jack Knebworth reckoned to have three fights a year. This was the third. The first had been with Stella, and the second had been with Stella, and the third was certainly to be with Stella.

"I wanted you to be here at ten. I've had these boys and girls waiting since a quarter of ten."

"What do you want to shoot?" she asked with an impatient jerk of her head.

"You mostly," said Jack slowly. "Get into No. 9 outfit and don't forget to leave your pearl earrings off. You're supposed to be a half-starved chorus girl. We're shooting at Griff Towers, and I told the gentleman who lent us the use of the house that I'd be through the day work by three. If you were Pauline Frederick or Norma Talmadge or Lillie Gish, you'd be worth waiting for, but Stella Mendoza has got to be on this lot by ten – and don't forget it!"

Old Jack Knebworth got up from his canvas chair and began to put on his coat with ominous deliberation, the flushed and angry girl watching him, her dark eyes blazing with injured pride and hurt vanity.

Stella had once been plain Maggie Stubbs, the daughter of a Midland grocer, and old Jack had talked to her as if she were still Maggie Stubbs and not the great film star of coruscating brilliance, idol (or her press agent lied) of the screen fans of all the world.

"All right, if you want a fuss you can have it, Knebworth. I'm going to quit – now! I think I know what is due to my position. That part's got to be rewritten to give me a chance of putting my personality over. There's too much leading man in it, anyway. People don't pay real money to see men. You don't treat me fair, Knebworth: I'm temper-amental, I admit it. You can't expect a woman of my kind to be a block of wood."

"The only thing about you that's a block of wood is your head, Stella," grunted the producer, and went on, oblivious to the rising fury expressed in the girl's face. "You've had two years playing small parts in Hollywood, and you've brought nothing back to England but a line of fresh talk, and you could have gotten that out of the Sunday supplements! Temperament! That's a word that means doctors' certificates when a picture's half taken, and a long rest unless your salary's put up fifty per cent. Thank God this picture isn't a quarter taken or an eighth. Quit, you mean-spirited guttersnipe – and quit as soon as you darn please!"

Boiling with rage, her lips quivering so that she could not articulate, the girl turned and flung out of the studio.

White-haired Jack Knebworth glared round at the silent company.

"This is where the miracle happens," he said sardonically. "This is where the extra girl who's left a sick mother and a mortgage at home leaps to fame in a night. If you don't know that kinder thing happens on every lot in Hollywood you're no students of fiction. Stand forth, Mary Pickford the second!"

The extras smiled, some amused, some uncomfortable, but none spoke. Adele was frozen stiff, incapable of speech.

"Modesty don't belong to this industry," old Jack sneered amiably. "Who thinks she can play 'Roselle' in this piece – because an extra's going to play the part, believe me! I'm going to show this pseudo-actress that there isn't an extra on this lot that couldn't play her head off. Somebody talked about playing a part yesterday – you!"

His forefinger pointed to Adele, and with a heart that beat tumultuously she went toward him.

"I had a camera test of you six months ago," said Jack suspiciously. "There was something wrong with her: what was it?"

He turned to his assistant. That young man scratched his head in an effort of memory.

"Ankles?" he hazarded a guess at random – a safe guess, for Knebworth had views about ankles.

"Nothing wrong with them – get out the print and let us see it."

Ten minutes later, Adele sat by the old man's side in the little projection room and saw her "test" run through.

"Hair!" said Knebworth triumphantly. "I knew there was something. Don't like bobbed hair. Makes a girl too pert and sophisticated. You've grown it?" he added as the lights were switched on.

"Yes, Mr Knebworth."

He looked at her in dispassionate admiration.

"You'll do," he said reluctantly. "See the wardrobe and get Miss Mendoza's costumes. There's one thing I'd like to tell you before you go," he said, stopping her. "You may be good and you may be bad, but, good or bad, there's no future for you – so don't get heated up. The only woman who's got any chance in England is the producer's wife, and I'll never marry you if you go down on your knees to me! That's the only kind of star they know in English films – the producer's wife; and unless you're that, you haven't –!"

He snapped his finger.

17

"I'll give you a word of advice, kid. If you make good in this picture, link yourself up with one of those cute English directors that set three flats and a pot of palms and call it a drawing-room! Give Miss What's-her-name the script, Harry. Say – go out somewhere quiet and study it, will you? Harry, you see the wardrobe. I give you half an hour to read that script!"

Like one in a dream, the girl walked out into the shady garden that ran the length of the studio building, and sat down, trying to concentrate on the typewritten lines. It wasn't true – it could not be true! And then she heard the crunch of feet on gravel and looked up in alarm. It was the young man who had seen her that morning – Michael Brixan.

"Oh, please – you mustn't interrupt me!" she begged in agitation. "I've got a part – a big part to read."

Her distress was so real that he hastened to take his departure.

"I'm awfully sorry – " he began.

In her confusion she had dropped the loose sheets of the manuscript, and, stooping with her to pick them up, their heads bumped.

"Sorry – that's an old comedy situation, isn't it?" he began.

And then he saw the sheet of paper in his hand and began to read. It was a page of elaborate description of a scene.

The cell is large, lighted by a swinging lamp. In centre is a steel gate through which a soldier on guard is seen pacing to and fro –

"Good God!" said Michael, and went white.

The "u's" in the type were blurred, the "g" was indistinct. The page had been typed on the machine from which the Head-Hunter sent forth his gruesome tales of death.

MR LAWLEY FOSS

"What is wrong?" asked Adele, seeing the young man's grave face.

"Where did this come from?"

He showed her the sheet of typewritten script.

"I don't know: it was with the other sheets. I knew, of course, that it didn't belong to 'Roselle.'"

"Is that the play you're acting in?" he asked quickly. And then: "Who would know?"

"Mr Knebworth."

"Where shall I find him?"

"You go through that door," she said, "and you will find him on the studio floor."

Without a word, he walked quickly into the building. Instinctively he knew which of the party was the man he sought. Jack Knebworth looked up under lowering brows at the sight of the stranger, for he was a stickler for privacy in business hours; but before he could demand an explanation, Michael was up to him.

"Are you Mr Knebworth?"

Jack nodded.

"I surely am," he said.

"May I speak to you for two minutes?"

"I can't speak to anybody for one minute," growled Jack. "Who are you, anyway, and who let you in?"

"I am a detective from the Foreign Office," said Michael, lowering his voice, and Jack's manner changed.

"Anything wrong?" he asked, as he accompanied the detective into his sanctum.

Jack laid down the sheet of paper with its typed characters on the table.

"Who wrote that?" he asked.

Jack Knebworth looked at the manuscript and shook his head.

"I've never seen it before. What is it all about?"

"You've never seen this manuscript at all?"

"No, I'll swear to that, but I dare say my scenario man will know all about it. I'll send for him."

He touched a bell, and, to the clerk who came: "Ask Mr Lawley Foss to come quickly," he said.

"The reading of books, plots and material for picture plays is entirely in the hands of my scenario manager," he said. "I never see a manuscript until he considers it's worth producing; and even then, of course, the picture isn't always made. If the story happens to be a bad one, I don't see it at all. I'm not so sure that I haven't lost some good stories, because Foss" – he hesitated a second – "well, he and I don't see exactly eye to eye. Now, Mr Brixan, what is the trouble?"

In a few words Michael explained the grave significance of the typewritten sheet.

"The Head-Hunter!" Jack whistled.

There came a knock at the door, and Lawley Foss slipped into the room. He was a thinnish man, dark and saturnine of face, shifty of eye. His face was heavily lined as though he suffered from some chronic disease. But the real disease which preyed on Lawley Foss was the bitterness of mind that comes to a man at war with the world. There had been a time in his early life when he thought that same world was at his feet. He had written two plays that had been produced and had run a few nights. Thereafter, he had trudged from theatre to theatre in vain, for the taint of failure was on him, and no manager would so much as open the brown-covered manuscripts he brought to them. Like many another man, he had sought easy ways to wealth, but the Stock Exchange and the race track had impoverished him still further.

He glanced suspiciously at Michael as he entered.

"I want to see you, Foss, about a sheet of script that's got amongst the 'Roselle' script," said Jack Knebworth. "May I tell Mr Foss what you have told me?"

Michael hesitated for a second. Some cautioning voice warned him to keep the question of the Head-Hunter a secret. Against his better judgment he nodded.

Lawley Foss listened with an expressionless face whilst the old director explained the significance of the interpolated sheet, then he took the page from Jack Knebworth's hand and examined it. Not by a twitch of his face or a droop of his eyelid did he betray his thoughts.

"I get a lot of stuff in," he said, "and I can't immediately place this particular play; but if you'll let me take it to my office, I will look up my books."

Again Michael considered. He did not wish that piece of evidence to pass out of his hands; and yet without confirmation and examination, it was fairly valueless. He reluctantly agreed.

"What do you make of that fellow?" asked Jack Knebworth when the door had closed upon the writer.

"I don't like him," said Michael bluntly. "In fact, my first impressions are distinctly unfavourable, though I am probably doing the poor gentleman a very great injustice."

Jack Knebworth sighed. Foss was one of his biggest troubles, sometimes bulking larger than the temperamental Mendoza.

"He certainly is a queer chap," he said, "though he's diabolically clever. I never knew a man who could take a plot and twist it as Lawley Foss can – but he's – difficult."

"I should imagine so," said Michael dryly.

They passed out into the studio, and Michael sought the troubled girl to explain his crudeness. There were tears of vexation in her eyes when he approached her, for his startling disappearance with a page of the script had put all thoughts of the play from her mind.

"I am sorry," he said penitently. "I almost wish I hadn't come."

"And I quite wish it," she said, smiling in spite of herself. "What was the matter with that page you took — you *are* a detective, aren't you?"

"I admit it!" said Michael recklessly.

"Did you speak the truth when you said that my uncle – " she stopped, at a loss for words.

"No, I did not," replied Michael quietly. "Your uncle is dead, Miss Leamington."

"Dead!" she gasped.

He nodded.

"He was murdered, in extraordinary circumstances."

Suddenly her face went white.

"He wasn't the man whose head was found at Esher?"

"How did you know?" he asked sharply.

"It was in this morning's newspaper," she said, and inwardly he cursed the sleuth-hound of a reporter who had got on to the track of this latest tragedy.

She had to know sooner or later: he satisfied himself with that thought.

The return of Foss relieved him of further explanations. The man spoke for a while with Jack Knebworth in a low voice, and then the director beckoned Michael across.

"Foss can't trace this manuscript," he said, handing back the sheet. "It may have been a sample page sent in by a contributor, or it may have been a legacy from our predecessors. I took over a whole lot of manuscript with the studio from a bankrupt production company."

He looked impatiently at his watch.

"Now, Mr Brixan, if it's possible I should be glad if you would excuse me. I've got some scenes to shoot ten miles away, with a leading lady from whose little head you've scared every idea that will be of the slightest value to me."

Michael acted upon an impulse.

"Would you mind my coming out with you to shoot — that means to photograph, doesn't it? I promise you I won't be in the way."

Old Jack nodded curtly, and ten minutes later Michael Brixan was sitting side by side with the girl in a char-à-banc which was carrying them to the location. That he should be riding with the artistes at all was a tribute to his nerve rather than to his modesty.

THE MASTER OF GRIFF

Adele did not speak to him for a long time. Resentment that he should force his company upon her, and nervousness at the coming ordeal – a nervousness which became sheer panic as they grew nearer and nearer to their destination – made conversation impossible.

"I see your Mr Lawley Foss is with us," said Michael, glancing over his shoulder, and by way of making conversation.

"He always goes on location," she said shortly. "A story has sometimes to be amended while it's being shot."

"Where are we going now?" he asked.

"Griff Towers first," she replied. She found it difficult to be uncivil to anybody. "It is a big place owned by Sir Gregory Penne."

"But I thought we were going to the Dower House?"

She looked at him with a little frown.

"Why did you ask if you knew?" she demanded, almost in a tone of asperity.

"Because I like to hear you speak," said the young man calmly. "Sir Gregory Penne? I seem to know the name."

She did not answer.

"He was in Borneo for many years, wasn't he?"

"He's hateful," she said vehemently. "I detest him!"

She did not explain the cause of her detestation, and Michael thought it discreet not to press the question, but presently she relieved him of responsibility.

"I've been to his house twice. He has a very fine garden, which Mr Knebworth has used before – of course, I only went as an extra and was very much in the background. I wish I had been more so. He has queer ideas about women, and especially actresses – not that I'm an actress," she added hastily, "but I mean people who play for a living. Thank heaven there's only one scene to be shot at Griff, and perhaps he will not be at home, but that's unlikely. He's always there when I go."

Michael glanced at her out of the corner of his eye. His first impression of her beauty was more than confirmed. There was a certain wistfulness in her face which was very appealing; an honesty in the dark eyes that told him all he wanted to know about her attitude toward the admiration of the unknown Sir Gregory.

"It's queer how all baronets are villains in stories," he said, "and queerer still that most of the baronets I've known have been men of singular morals. I'm bothering you, being here, aren't I?" he asked, dropping his tone of banter.

She looked round at him.

"You are a little," she said frankly. "You see, Mr Brixan, this is my big chance. It's a chance that really never comes to an extra except in stories, and I'm frightened to death of what is going to happen. You make me nervous, but what makes me more panic-stricken is that the first scene is to be shot at Griff. I hate it, I hate it!" she said almost savagely. "That big, hard-looking house, with its hideous stuffed tigers and its awful looking swords – "

"Swords?" he asked quickly. "What do you mean?"

"The walls are covered with them – Eastern swords. They make me shiver to see them. But Sir Gregory takes a delight in them: he told Mr Knebworth, the last time we were there, that the swords were as sharp now as they were when they came from the hands of their makers, and some of them were three hundred years old. He's an extraordinary man: he can cut an apple in half on your hand and never so much as scratch you. That is one of his favourite stunts – do you know what 'stunt' means?"

"I seem to have heard the expression," said Michael absently.

"There is the house," she pointed. "Ugh! It makes me shiver."

Griff Towers was one of those bleak looking buildings that it had been the delight of the early Victorian architects to erect. Its one grey tower, placed on the left wing, gave it a lopsided appearance, but even this distortion did not distract attention from its rectangular unloveliness. The place seemed all the more bare, since the walls were innocent of greenery, and it stood starkly in the midst of a yellow expanse of gravel.

"Looks almost like a barracks," said Michael, "with a parade ground in front!"

They passed through the lodge gates, and the char-à-banc stopped halfway up the drive. The gardens apparently were in the rear of the building, and certainly there was nothing that would attract the most careless of directors in its uninteresting façade.

Michael got down from his seat and found Jack Knebworth already superintending the unloading of a camera and reflectors. Behind the char-à-banc came the big dynamo lorry, with three sun arcs that were to enhance the value of daylight.

"Oh, you're here, are you?" growled Jack. "Now you'll oblige me, Mr Brixan, by not getting in the way? I've got a hard morning's work ahead of me."

"I want you to take me on as a – what is the word? – extra," said Michael.

The old man frowned at him.

"Say, what's the great idea?" he asked suspiciously.

"I have an excellent reason, and I promise you that nothing I do will in any way embarrass you. The truth is, Mr Knebworth, I want to be around for the remainder of the day, and I need an excuse."

Jack Knebworth bit his lip, scratched his long chin, scowled, and then: "All right," he said gruffly. "Maybe you'll come in handy, though I'll have quite enough bother directing one amateur, and if you get into the pictures on this trip you're going to be lucky!"

There was a man of the party, a tall young man whose hair was brushed back from his forehead, and was so tidy and well arranged that it seemed as if it had originally been stuck by glue and varnished over. A tall, somewhat good-looking boy, who had sat on Adele's left throughout the journey and had not spoken once, he raised his eyebrows at the appearance of Michael, and, strolling across to the harassed Knebworth, his hands in his pockets, he asked with a hurt air: "I say, Mr Knebworth, who is this johnny?"

"Which johnny?" growled old Jack. "You mean Brixan? He's an extra."

"Oh, an extra, is he?" said the young man. "I say, it's pretty desperately awful when extras hobnob with principals! And this Leamington girl – she's simply going to mess up the pictures, she is, by Jove!"

"Is she, by Jove?" snarled Knebworth. "Now see here, Mr Connolly, I ain't so much in love with your work that I'm willing to admit in advance that even an extra is going to mess up this picture."

"I've never played opposite to an extra in my life, dash it all!"

"Then you must have felt lonely," grunted Jack, busy with his unpacking.

"Now, Mendoza is an artiste – " began the youthful leading man, and Jack Knebworth straightened his back.

"Get over there till you're wanted, you!" he roared. "When I need advice from pretty boys, I'll come to you – see? For the moment you're *de trop*, which is a French expression meaning that you're standing on ground there's a better use for."

The disgruntled Reggie Connolly strolled away with a shrug of his thin shoulders, which indicated not only his conviction that the picture would fail, but that the responsibility was everywhere but under his hat.

From the big doorway of Griff Towers, Sir Gregory Penne was watching the assembly of the company. He was a thick-set man, and the sun of Borneo and an unrestricted appetite had dyed his skin a colour which was between purple and brown. His face was covered with innumerable ridges, his eyes looked forth upon the world through two narrow slits. The rounded feminine chin seemed to be the only part of his face that sunshine and stronger stimulants had left in its natural condition.

Michael watched him as he strolled down the slope to where they were standing, guessing his identity. He wore a golf suit of a loud check in which red predominated, and a big cap of the same material was pulled down over his eyes. Taking the stub of a cigar from his teeth, with a quick and characteristic gesture he wiped his scanty moustache on his knuckles.

"Good morning, Knebworth," he called.

His voice was harsh and cruel; a voice that had never been mellowed by laughter or made soft by the tendernesses of humanity.

"Good morning, Sir Gregory."

Old Knebworth disentangled himself from his company.

"Sorry I'm late."

"Don't apologize," said the other. "Only I thought you were going to shoot earlier. Brought my little girl, eh?"

"Your little girl?" Jack looked at him, frankly nonplussed. "You mean Mendoza? No, she's not coming."

"I don't mean Mendoza, if that's the dark girl. Never mind: I was only joking."

Who the blazes was his little girl, thought Jack, who was ignorant of two unhappy experiences which an unconsidered extra girl had had on previous visits. The mystery, however, was soon cleared up, for the baronet walked slowly to where Adele Leamington was making a pretence of studying her script.

"Good morning, little lady," he said, lifting his cap an eighth of an inch from his head.

"Good morning, Sir Gregory," she said coldly.

"You didn't keep your promise." He shook his head waggishly. "Oh, woman, woman!"

"I don't remember having made a promise," said the girl quietly. "You asked me to come to dinner with you, and I told you that that was impossible."

"I promised to send my car for you. Don't say it was too far away. Never mind, never mind." And, to Michael's wrath, he squeezed the girl's arm in a manner which was intended to be paternal, but which filled the girl with indignant loathing.

She wrenched her arm free, and, turning her back upon her tormentor, almost flew to Jack Knebworth with an incoherent demand for information on the reading of a line which was perfectly simple.

Old Jack was no fool. He watched the play from under his eyelids, recognizing all the symptoms.

"This is the last time we shall shoot at Griff Towers," he told himself.

For Jack Knebworth was something of a stickler on behaviour, and had views on women which were diametrically opposite to those held by Sir Gregory Penne.

THE SWORDS AND BHAG

The little party moved away, leaving Michael alone with the baronet. For a period, Gregory Penne watched the girl, his eyes glittering; then he became aware of Michael's presence and turned a cold, insolent stare upon the other.

"What are you?" he asked, looking the detective up and down.

"I'm an extra," said Michael.

"An extra, eh? Sort of chorus boy? Put paint and powder on your face and all that sort of thing? What a life for a man!"

"There are worse," said Michael, holding his antagonism in check.

"Do you know that little girl – what's her name, Leamington?" asked the baronet suddenly.

"I know her extremely well," said Michael untruthfully.

"Oh, you do, eh?" said the master of Griff Towers with sudden amiability. "She's a nice little thing. Quite a cut above the ordinary chorus girl. You might bring her along to dinner one night. She'd come with you, eh?"

The contortions of the puffy eyelids suggested to Michael that the man had winked. There was something about this gross figure that interested the scientist in Michael Brixan. He was elemental; an animal invested with a brain; and yet he must be something more than that if he had held a high administrative position under Government.

"Are you acting? If you're not, you can come up and have a look at my swords," said the man suddenly.

Michael guessed that, for a reason of his own, probably because of his claim to be Adele's friend, the man wished to cultivate the acquaintance.

"No, I'm not acting," replied Michael.

And no invitation could have given him greater pleasure. Did their owner realize the fact, Michael Brixan had already made up his mind not to leave Griff Towers until he had inspected that peculiar collection.

"Yes, she's a nice little girl."

Penne returned to the subject immediately as they paced up the slope toward the house.

"As I say, a cut above chorus girls. Young, unsophisticated, virginal! You can have your sophisticated girls: there is no mystery to 'em! They revolt me. A girl should be like a spring flower. Give me the violet and the snowdrop: you can have a bushel of cabbage roses for one petal of the shy dears of the forest."

Michael listened with a keen sense of nausea, and yet with an unusual interest, as the man rambled on. He said things which were sickening, monstrous. There were moments when Brixan found it difficult to keep his hands off the obscene figure that paced at his side; and only by adopting toward him the attitude with which the enthusiastic naturalist employs in his dealings with snakes, was he able to get a grip of himself.

The big entrance hall into which he was ushered was paved with earthen tiles, and, looking up at the stone walls, Michael had his first glimpse of the famous swords.

There were hundreds of them – poniards, scimitars, ancient swords of Japan, basket-hilted hangers, two-handed swords that had felt the grip of long-dead Crusaders.

"What do you think of 'em, eh?" Sir Gregory Penne spoke with the pride of an enthusiastic collector. "There isn't one of them that could be duplicated, my boy; and they're only the rag, tag and bobtail of my collection."

He led his visitor along a broad corridor, lighted by square windows set at intervals, and here again the walls were covered with shining weapons. Throwing open a door, Sir Gregory ushered the other into a large room which was evidently his library, though the books were few, and, so far as Michael could see at first glance, the conventional volumes that are to be found in the houses of the country gentry.

Over the mantelshelf were two great swords of a pattern which Michael did not remember having seen before.

"What do you think of those?"

Penne lifted one from the silver hook which supported it, and drew it from its scabbard.

"Don't feel the edge unless you want to cut yourself. This would split a hair, but it would also cut you in two, and you would never know what had happened till you fell apart!"

Suddenly his manner changed, and he almost snatched the sword from Michael's hand, and, putting it back in its sheath, he hung it up.

"That is a Sumatran sword, isn't it?"

"It comes from Borneo," said the baronet shortly.

"The home of the head-hunters."

Sir Gregory looked round, his brows lowered. "No," he said, "it comes from Dutch Borneo."

Evidently there was something about this weapon which aroused unpleasant memories. He glowered for a long time in silence into the little fire that was burning on the hearth.

"I killed the man who owned that," he said at last, and it struck Michael that he was speaking more to himself than to his visitor. "At least, I hope I killed him. I hope so!"

He glanced round, and Michael Brixan could have sworn there was apprehension in his eyes.

"Sit down, What's-your-name," he commanded, pointing to a low settee. "We'll have a drink."

He pushed a bell, and, to Michael's astonishment, the summons was answered by an undersized native, a little copper-coloured man, naked to the waist. Gregory gave an order in a language which was unintelligible to Michael – he guessed, by its sibilants, it was Malayan – and the servant, with a quick salaam, disappeared, and came back almost instantly with a tray containing a large decanter and two thin glasses.

"I have no white servants – can't stand 'em," said Penne, taking the contents of his glass at a gulp. "I like servants who don't steal and don't gossip. You can lick 'em if they misbehave, and there's no trouble. I got this fellow last year in Sumatra, and he's the best butler I've had."

"Do you go to Borneo every year?" asked Michael.

"I go almost every year," said the other. "I've got a yacht: she's lying at Southampton now. If I didn't get out of this cursed country once a year, I'd go mad. There's nothing here, nothing! Have you ever met that dithering old fool, Longvale? Knebworth said you were going on to him – pompous old ass, who lives in the past and dresses like an advertisement for somebody's whisky. Have another?"

"I haven't finished this yet," said Michael with a smile, and his eyes went up to the sword above the mantelpiece. "Have you had that very long? It looks modern."

"It isn't," snapped the other. "Modern! It's three hundred years old if it's a day. I've only had it a year." Again he changed the subject abruptly. "I like you, What's-your-name. I like people or I dislike them instantly. You're the sort of fellow who'd do well in the East. I've made two millions there. The East is full of wonder, full of unbelievable things." He screwed his head round and fixed Michael with a glittering eye. "Full of good servants," he said slowly. "Would you like to meet the perfect servant?"

There was something peculiar in his tone, and Michael nodded.

"Would you like to see the slave who never asks questions and never disobeys, who has no love but love of me" – he thumped himself on the chest – "no hate but for the people I hate – my trusty – Bhag?"

He rose, and, crossing to his table, turned a little switch that Michael had noticed attached to the side of the desk. As he did so, a part of the panelled wall at the farther end of the room swung open. For a second Michael saw nothing, and then there emerged, blinking into the daylight, a most sinister, a most terrifying figure. And Michael Brixan had need for all his self-control to check the exclamation that rose to his lips.

BHAG

It was a great orang-outang. Crouched as it was, gazing malignantly upon the visitor with its bead-like eyes, it stood over six feet in height. The hairy chest was enormous; the arms that almost touched the floor were as thick as an average man's thigh. It wore a pair of workman's dark blue overalls, held in place by two straps that crossed the broad shoulders.

"Bhag!" called Sir Gregory in a voice so soft that Michael could not believe it was the man's own. "Come here."

The gigantic figure waddled across the room to where they stood before the fireplace.

"This is a friend of mine, Bhag."

The great ape held out his hand, and for a second Michael's was held in its velvet palm. This done, he lifted his paw to his nose and sniffed loudly, the only sound he made.

"Get me some cigars," said Penne.

Immediately the ape walked to a cabinet, pulled open a drawer, and brought out a box.

"Not those," said Gregory. "The small ones."

He spoke distinctly, as if he were articulating to somebody who was deaf, and, without a moment's hesitation, the hideous Bhag replaced the box and brought out another.

"Pour me out a whisky and soda."

The ape obeyed. He did not spill a drop, and when his owner said "Enough," replaced the stopper in the decanter and put it back.

"Thank you, that will do, Bhag."

Without a sound the ape waddled back to the open panelling and disappeared, and the door closed behind him.

"Why, the thing is human," said Michael in an awe-stricken whisper.

Sir Gregory Penne chuckled.

"More than human," he said. "Bhag is my shield against all trouble."

His eyes seemed to go instantly to the sword above the mantelpiece.

"Where does he live?"

"He's got a little apartment of his own, and he keeps it clean. He feeds with the servants."

"Good Lord!" gasped Michael, and the other chuckled again at the surprise he had aroused.

"Yes, he feeds with the servants. They're afraid of him, but they worship him: he's a sort of god to them, but they're afraid of him. Do you know what would have happened if I'd said 'This man is my enemy?'" He pointed his stubby finger at Michael's chest. "He would have torn you limb from limb. You wouldn't have had a chance, Mr What's-your-name, not a dog's chance. And yet he can be gentle – yes, he can be gentle." He nodded. "And cunning! He goes out almost every night, and I've had no complaints from the villagers. No sheep stolen, nobody frightened. He just goes out and loafs around in the woods, and doesn't kill as much as a hen partridge."

"How long have you had him?"

"Eight or nine years," said the baronet carelessly, swallowing the whisky that the ape had poured for him. "Now let's go out and see the actors and actresses. She's a nice girl, eh? You're not forgetting you're going to bring her to dinner, are you? What is your name?"

"Brixan," said Michael. "Michael Brixan."

Sir Gregory grunted something.

"I'll remember that – Brixan. I ought to have told Bhag. He likes to know."

"Would he have known me again, suppose you had?" asked Michael, smiling.

"Known you?" said the baronet contemptuously. "He will not only know you, but he'll be able to trail you down. Notice him smelling his hand? He was filing you for reference, my boy. If I told him 'Go along and take this message to Brixan,' he'd find you."

When they reached the lovely gardens at the back of the house, the first scene had been shot, and there was a smile on Jack Knebworth's face which suggested that Adele's misgivings had not been justified. And so it proved.

"That girl's a peach," Jack unbent to say. "A natural born actress, built for this scene – it's almost too good to be true. What do you want?"

It was Mr Reggie Connolly, and he had the obsession which is perpetual in every leading man. He felt that sufficient opportunities had not been offered to him.

"I say, Mr Knebworth," he said in a grieved tone, "I'm not getting much of the fat in this story! So far, there's about thirty feet of me in this picture. I say, that's not right, you know! If a johnny is being featured – "

"You're not being featured," said Jack shortly. "And Mendoza's chief complaint was that there was too much of you in it."

Michael looked round. Sir Gregory Penne had strolled toward where the girl was standing, and, in her state of elation, she had no room in her heart even for resentment against the man she so cordially detested.

"Little girl, I want to speak to you before you go," he said, dropping his voice, and for once she smiled at him.

"Well, you have a good opportunity now, Sir Gregory," she said.

"I want to tell you how sorry I am for what happened the other day, and I respect you for what you said, for a girl's entitled to keep her kisses for men she likes. Aren't I right?"

"Of course you're right," she said. "Please don't think any more about it, Sir Gregory."

"I'd no right to kiss you against your will, especially when you're in my house. Are you going to forgive me?"

"I do forgive you," she said, and would have left him, but he caught her arm.

"You're coming to dinner, aren't you?" He jerked his head toward the watchful Michael. "Your friend said he'd bring you along."

"Which friend?" she asked, her eyebrows raised. "You mean Mr Brixan?"

"That's the fellow. Why do you make friends with that kind of man? Not that he isn't a decent fellow. I like him personally. Will you come along to dinner?"

"I'm afraid I can't," she said, her old aversion gaining ground.

"Little girl," he said earnestly, "there's nothing you couldn't have from me. Why do you want to trouble your pretty head about this cheap play acting? I'll give you a company of your own if you want it, and the best car that money can buy."

His eyes were like points of fire, and she shivered.

"I have all I want, Sir Gregory," she said.

She was furious with Michael Brixan. How dare he presume to accept an invitation on her behalf? How dare he call himself her friend? Her anger almost smothered her dislike for her persecutor.

"You come over tonight – let him bring you," said Penne huskily. "I want you tonight – do you hear? You're staying at old Longvale's. You can easily slip out."

"I'll do nothing of the kind. I don't think you know what you're asking, Sir Gregory," she said quietly. "Whatever you mean, it is an insult to me."

Turning abruptly, she left him. Michael would have spoken to her, but she passed, her head in the air, a look on her face which dismayed him, though, after a moment's consideration, he could guess the cause.

When the various apparatus was packed, and the company had taken their seats in the char-à-banc, Michael observed that she had very carefully placed herself between Jack Knebworth and the sulking leading man, and wisely himself chose a seat some distance from her.

The car was about to start when Sir Gregory came up to him, and, stepping on the running. board: "You said you'd get her over – " he began.

"If I said that," said Michael, "I must have been drunk, and it takes more than one glass of whisky to reduce me to that disgusting condition. Miss Leamington is a free agent, and she would be singularly ill-advised to dine alone with you or any other man."

He expected an angry outburst, but, to his surprise, the squat man only laughed and waved him a pleasant farewell. Looking round as the car turned from the lodge gates, Michael saw him standing on the lawn, talking to a man, and recognized Foss, who, for some reason, had stayed behind.

And then his eyes strayed past the two men to the window of the library, where the monstrous Bhag sat in his darkened room, waiting for instructions which he would carry into effect without reason or pity. Michael Brixan, hardened as he was to danger of every variety, found himself shuddering.

THE ANCESTOR

The Dower House was away from the main road. A sprawling mass of low buildings, it stood behind untidy hedges and crumbling walls. Once the place had enjoyed the services of a lodge-keeper, but the tiny lodge was deserted, the windows broken, and there were gaps in the tiled roof. The gates had not been closed for generations; they were broken, and leant crazily against the walls to which they had been thrust by the last person who had employed them to guard the entrance to the Dower House.

What had once been a fair lawn was now a tangle of weeds. Thistle and mayweed grew knee-deep where the gallants of old had played their bowls; and it was clear to Michael, from his one glance, that only a portion of the house was used. In only one of the wings were the windows whole; the others were broken or so grimed with dirt, that they appeared to have been painted.

His amusement blended with curiosity, Michael saw for the first time the picturesque Mr Sampson Longvale. He came out to meet them, his bald head glistening in the afternoon sunlight, his strapped fawn-coloured trousers, velvet waistcoat and old-fashioned stock completely supporting Gregory Penne's description of him.

"Delighted to see you, Mr Knebworth. I've a very poor house, but I offer you a very rich welcome! I have had tea served in my little dining-room. Will you please introduce me to the members of your company?"

The courtesy, the old-world spirit of dignity, were very charming, and Michael felt a warm glow toward this fine old man who brought to this modern atmosphere the love and the fragrance of a past age.

"I should like to shoot a scene before we lose the light, Mr Longvale," said Knebworth, "so, if you don't mind the meal being a scrambling one, I can give the company a quarter of an hour." He looked round. "Where is Foss?" he asked. "I want to change a scene."

"Mr Foss said he was walking from Griff Towers," said one of the company. "He stopped behind to speak to Sir Gregory."

Jack Knebworth cursed his dilatory scenario man with vigour and originality.

"I hope he hasn't stopped to borrow money," he said savagely. "That fellow's going to ruin my credit if I'm not careful."

He had overcome his objection to his new extra; possibly he felt that there was nobody else in the party whom he could take into his confidence without hurt to discipline.

"Is he that way inclined?"

"He's always short of money and always trying to make it by some fool trick which leaves him shorter than he was before. When a man gets that kind of bug in his head he's only a block away from prison. Are you going to stay the night? I don't think you'll be able to sleep here," he said, changing the subject, "but I suppose you'll be going back to London?"

"Not tonight," said Michael quickly. "Don't worry about me. I particularly do not wish to give you any trouble."

"Come and meet the old man," said Knebworth under his breath. "He's a queer old devil with the heart of a child."

"I like what I've seen of him," said Michael. Mr Longvale accepted the introduction all over again.

"I fear there will not be sufficient room in my dining-room for the whole company. I have had a little table laid in my study. Perhaps you and your friends would like to have your tea there?"

"Why, that's very kind of you, Mr Longvale. You have met Mr Brixan?"

The old man smiled and nodded.

"I have met him without realizing that I've met him. I never remember names – a curious failing which was shared by my great-great-uncle Charles, with the result that he fell into extraordinary confusion when he wrote his memoirs, and in consequence many of the incidents he relates have been regarded as apocryphal."

He showed them into a narrow room that ran from the front to the back of the house. Its ceilings were supported by black rafters; the open wainscoting, polished and worn by generations of hands, must have been at least five hundred years old. There were no swords over this mantelpiece, thought Michael with an inward smile. Instead, there was a portrait of a handsome old gentleman, the dignity of whose face was arresting. There was only one word with an adequate description: it was majestic.

He made no comment on the picture, nor did the old man speak of it till later. The meal was hastily disposed of, and, sitting on the wall, Michael watched the last daylight scene shot, and was struck by the plastic genius of the girl. He knew enough of motion pictures and their construction to realize what it meant to the director to have in his hands one who could so faithfully reproduce the movements and the emotions which the old man dictated.

In other circumstances he might have thought it grotesque to see Jack Knebworth pretending to be a young girl, resting his elderly cheek coyly upon the back of his clasped hand, and walking with mincing steps from one side of the picture to the other. But he knew that the American was a mason who was cutting roughly the shape of the sculpture and leaving it to the finer artiste to express in her personality the delicate contours that would delight the eye of the picture-loving world. She was no longer Adele Leamington; she was Roselle, the heiress to an estate of which her wicked cousin was trying to deprive her. The story itself he recognized; a half-and-half plagiarism of "The Cat and the Canary," with which were blended certain situations from "The Miracle Man." He mentioned this fact when the scene was finished.

"I guess it's a steal," said Jack Knebworth philosophically, "and I didn't inquire too closely into it. It's Foss' story, and I should be pained to discover there was anything original in it."

Mr Foss had made a tardy reappearance, and Michael found himself wondering what was the nature of that confidential interview which the writer had had with Sir Gregory.

Going back to the long sitting-room, he stood watching the daylight fade and speculating upon the one mystery within a mystery – the extraordinary effect which Adele had produced upon him.

Mike Brixan had known many beautiful women, women in every class of society. He had known the best and the worst, he had jailed a few, and had watched one face a French firing squad one grey wintry morning at Vincennes. He had liked many, nearly loved one, and it seemed, cold-bloodedly analysing his emotions, that he was in danger of actually loving a girl whom he had never met before that morning.

"Which is absurd," he said aloud.

"What is absurd?" asked Knebworth, who had come into the room unnoticed.

"I also wondered what you were thinking," smiled old Mr Longvale, who had been watching the young man in silence.

"I – er – well, I was thinking of the portrait." Michael turned and indicated the picture above the fireplace, and in a sense he spoke the truth, for the thread of that thought had run through all others. "The face seemed familiar," he said, "which is absurd, because it is obviously an old painting."

Mr Longvale lit two candles and carried one to the portrait. Again Michael looked, and again the majesty of the face impressed him.

"That is my great-great-uncle, Charles Henry," said old Mr Longvale with pride. "Or, as we call him affectionately in our family, the Great Monsieur."

Michael's face was half-turned toward the window as the old man spoke... Suddenly the room seemed to spin before his eyes. Jack Knebworth saw his face go white and caught him by the arm.

"What's the matter?" he asked.

"Nothing," said Michael unsteadily.

Knebworth was staring past him at the window.

"What was that?" he said.

With the exception of the illumination from the two candles and the faint dusk light that came from the garden, the room was in darkness.

"Did you see it?" he asked, and ran to the window, staring out.

"What was it?" asked old Mr Longvale, joining him.

"I could have sworn I saw a head in the window. Did you see it, Brixan?"

"I saw something," said Michael unsteadily. "Do you mind if I go out into the garden?"

"I hoped you saw it. It looked like a monkey's head to me."

Michael nodded. He walked down the flagged passage into the garden, and, as he did so, slipped a Browning from his hip, pressed down the safety catch, and dropped the pistol into his jacket pocket.

He disappeared, and five minutes later Knebworth saw him pacing the garden path, and went out to him.

"Did you see anything?"

"Nothing in the garden. You must have been mistaken."

"But didn't you see him?"

Michael hesitated.

"I thought I saw something," he said with an assumption of carelessness. "When are you going to shoot those night pictures of yours?"

"You saw something, Brixan – was it a face?"

Mike Brixan nodded.

THE OPEN WINDOW

The dynamo wagon was humming as he walked down the garden path, and with a hiss and a splutter from the arcs, the front of the cottage was suddenly illuminated by their fierce light. Outside on the road a motorist had pulled up to look upon the unusual spectacle.

"What is happening?" he asked curiously.

"They're taking a picture," said Michael.

"Oh, is that what it is? I suppose it is one of Knebworth's outfits?"

"Where are you going?" demanded Michael suddenly. "Forgive my asking you, but if you're heading for Chichester you can render me a very great service if you give me a lift."

"Jump in," said the man. "I'm going to Petworth, but it will not be much out of my way to take you into the city."

Until they came to the town he plied Michael with questions betraying that universal inquisitiveness which picture-making invariably incites amongst the uninitiated.

Michael got down near the market-place and made his way to the house of a man he knew, a former master at his old school, now settled down in Chichester, who had, amongst other possessions, an excellent library. Declining his host's pressing invitation to dinner, Michael stated his needs, and the old master laughed.

"I can't remember that you were much of a student in my days, Michael," he said, "but you may have the run of the library. Is it some line of Virgil that escapes you? I may be able to save you a hunt."

"It's not Virgil, maestro," smiled Michael. "Something infinitely more full-blooded!"

He was in the library for twenty minutes, and when he emerged there was a light of triumph in his eye.

"I'm going to use your telephone if I may," he said, and he got London without delay.

For ten minutes he was speaking with Scotland Yard, and, when he had finished, he went into the dining-room where the master, who was a bachelor, was eating his solitary dinner.

"You can render me one more service, mentor of my youth," he said. "Have you in this abode of peace an automatic pistol that throws a heavier shell than this?"

And he put his own on the table. Michael knew Mr Scott had been an officer of the Territorial Army, and incidentally an instructor of the Officers' Training Corps, so that his request was not as impossible of fulfilment as it appeared.

"Yes, I can give you a heavier one than that. What are you shooting – elephants?"

"Something a trifle more dangerous," said Michael.

"Curiosity was never a weakness of mine," said the master, and went out to return with a Browning of heavy calibre and a box of cartridges.

They spent five minutes cleaning the pistol, which had not been in use for some time, and, with his new weapon weighing down his jacket pocket, Mike took his leave, carrying a lighter heart and a clearer understanding than he had enjoyed when he had arrived at the house.

He hired a car from a local garage and drove back to the Dower House, dismissing the car just short of his destination. Jack Knebworth had not even noticed that he had disappeared. But old Mr Longvale, wearing a coat with many capes, and a soft silk cap from which dangled a long tassel, came to him almost as soon as he entered the garden.

"May I speak to you, Mr Brixan?" he said in a low voice, and they went into the house together. "Do you remember Mr Knebworth was very perturbed because he thought he saw somebody peering in at the window – something with a monkey's head?"

46

Michael nodded.

"Well, it is a most curious fact," said the old gentleman impressively, "that a quarter of an hour ago I happened to be walking in the far end of my garden, and, looking across the hedge toward the field, I suddenly saw a gigantic form rise, apparently from the ground, and move toward these bushes" – he pointed through the window to a clump in a field on the opposite side of the road. "He seemed to be crouching forward and moving furtively."

"Will you show me the place?" said Michael quickly.

He followed the other across the road to the bushes, a little clump which was empty when they reached it. Kneeling down to make a new skyline, Michael scanned the limited horizon, but there was no sign of Bhag. For that it was Bhag he had no doubt. There might be nothing in it. Penne told him that the animal was in the habit of taking nightly strolls, and that he was perfectly harmless. Suppose...

The thought was absurd, fantastically absurd. And yet the animal had been so extraordinarily human that no speculation in connection with it was quite absurd.

When he returned to the garden, he went in search of the girl. She had finished her scene and was watching the stealthy movements of two screen burglars, who were creeping along the wall in the subdued light of the arcs.

"Excuse me, Miss Leamington, I'm going to ask you an impertinent question. Have you brought a complete change of clothes with you?"

"Why ever do you ask that?" she demanded, her eyes wide open. "Of course I did! I always bring a complete change in case the weather breaks."

"That's one question. Did you lose anything when you were at Griff Towers?"

"I lost my gloves," she said quickly. "Did you find them?"

"No. When did you miss them?"

"I missed them immediately. I thought for a moment – " She stopped. "It was a foolish idea, but – "

"What did you think?" he asked.

"I'd rather not tell you. It is a purely personal matter."

"You thought that Sir Gregory had taken them as a souvenir?"

Even in the half-darkness he saw her colour come and go.

"I did think that," she said, a little stiffly.

"Then it doesn't matter very much – about your change of clothing," he said.

"Whatever are you talking about?"

She looked at him suspiciously. He guessed she thought that he had been drinking, but the last thing in the world he wanted to do at that moment was to explain his somewhat disjointed questions.

"Now everybody is going to bed!"

It was old Jack Knebworth talking.

"Everybody! Off you go! Mr Foss has shown you your rooms. I want you up at four o'clock tomorrow morning, so get as much sleep as you can. Foss, you've marked the rooms?"

"Yes," said the man. "I've put the names on every door. I've given this young lady a room to herself – is that right?"

"I suppose it is," said Knebworth dubiously. "Anyway, she won't be there long enough to get used to it."

The girl said good night to the detective and went straight up to her apartment. It was a tiny room, smelling somewhat musty, and was simply furnished. A truckle bed, a chest of drawers with a swinging glass on top, and a small table and chair was all that the apartment contained. By the light of her candle, the floor showed signs of having been recently scrubbed, and the centre was covered by a threadbare square of carpet.

She locked the door, blew out the candle and, undressing in the dark, went to the window and threw open the casement. And then, for the first time, she saw, on the centre of one of the small panes, a circular disc of paper. It was pasted on the outside of the window, and at first she was about to pull it off, when she guessed that it might be some indicator placed by Knebworth to mark an exact position that he required for the morning picture-taking.

She did not immediately fall asleep, her mind for some curious reason, being occupied unprofitably with a tumultuous sense of annoyance directed towards Michael Brixan. For a long time a strong sense of justice fought with a sense of humour equally powerful. He was a nice man, she told herself; the sixth sense of woman had already delivered that information, heavily underlined. He certainly had nerve. In the end humour brought sleep. She was smiling when her eyelids closed.

She had been sleeping two hours, though it did not seem two seconds. A sense of impending danger wakened her, and she sat up in bed, her heart thumping wildly. She looked round the room. In the pale moonlight she could see almost every corner, and it was empty. Was it somebody outside the door that had wakened her? She tried the door handle: it was locked, as she had left it. The window? It was very near to the ground, she remembered. Stepping to the window, she pulled one casement close. She was closing the other when, out of the darkness below, reached a great hairy arm and a hand closed like a vice on her wrist.

She did not scream. She stood breathless, dying of terror, she felt. Her heart ceased beating, and she was conscious of a deadly cold. What was it? What could it be? Summoning all her courage, she looked out of the window down into a hideous, bestial face and two round, green eyes that stared into hers.

THE MARK ON THE WINDOW

The thing was twittering at her, soft, birdlike noises, and she saw the flash of its white teeth in the darkness. It was not pulling, it was simply holding, one hand gripping the tendrils of the ivy up which it had climbed, the other hand firmly about her wrist. Again it twittered and pulled. She drew back, but she might as well have tried to draw back from a moving piston rod. A great, hairy leg was suddenly flung over the sill; the second hand came up and covered her face.

The sound of her scream was deadened in the hairy paw, but somebody heard it. From the ground below came a flash of fire and the deafening 'tang!' of a pistol exploding. A bullet zipped and crashed amongst the ivy, striking the brickwork, and she heard the whirr of the ricochet. Instantly the great monkey released his hold and dropped down out of sight. Half swooning, she dropped upon the window-sill, incapable of movement. And then she saw a figure come out of the shadow of the laurel bush, and instantly recognized the midnight prowler. It was Michael Brixan.

"Are you hurt?" he asked in a low voice.

She could only shake her head, for speech was denied her.

"I didn't hit him, did I?"

With an effort she found a husk of a voice in her dry throat.

"No, I don't think so. He dropped."

Michael had pulled an electric torch from his pocket and was searching the ground.

"No sign of blood. He was rather difficult to hit – I was afraid of hurting you, too."

A window had been thrown up and Jack Knebworth's voice bawled into the night.

"What's the shooting? Is that you, Brixan?"

"It is I. Come down, and I'll tell you all about it."

The noise did not seem to have aroused Mr Longvale, or, for the matter of that, any other member of the party; and when Knebworth reached the garden, he found no other audience than Mike Brixan.

In a few words Michael told him what he had seen.

"The monkey belongs to friend Penne," he said. "I saw it this morning."

"What do you think – that he was prowling round and saw the open window?"

Michael shook his head.

"No," he said quietly, "he came with one intention and purpose, which was to carry off your leading lady. That sounds highly dramatic and improbable, and that is the opinion I have formed. This ape, I tell you, is nearly human."

"But he wouldn't know the girl. He has never seen her."

"He could smell her," said Mike instantly. "She lost a pair of gloves at the Towers today, and it's any odds that they were stolen by the noble Gregory Penne, so that he might introduce to Bhag an unfailing scent."

"I can't believe it; it is incredible! Though I'll admit," said Jack Knebworth thoughtfully, "that these big apes do some amazing things. Did you shoot him?"

"No, sir, I didn't shoot him, but I can tell you this, that he's an animal that's been gunned before, or he'd have come for me, in which case he would have been now fairly dead."

"What were you doing round here, anyway?"

"Just watching out," said the other carelessly. "The earnest detective has so many things on his conscience that he can't sleep like ordinary people. Speaking for myself, I never intended leaving the garden, because I expected Brer Bhag. Who is that?"

The door opened, and a slim figure, wrapped in a dressing-gown, came out into the open.

"Young lady, you're going to catch a very fine cold," warned Knebworth. "What happened to you?"

"I don't know." She was feeling her wrist tenderly. "I heard something and went to the window, and then this horrible thing caught hold of me. What was it, Mr Brixan?"

"It was nothing more alarming than a monkey," said he with affected unconcern.

"I'm sorry you were so scared. I guess the shooting worried you more?"

"You don't guess anything of the kind. You know it didn't. Oh, it was horrible, horrible!" She covered her face with her trembling hands.

Old Jack grunted.

"I think she's right, too. You owe something to our friend here, young lady. Apparently he was expecting this visit and watched in the garden."

"You expected it?" she gasped.

"Mr Knebworth has made rather more of the part I played than can be justified," said Mike. "And if you think that this is a hero's natural modesty, you're mistaken. I did expect this gentleman, because he'd been seen in the fields by Mr Longvale. And you thought you saw him yourself, didn't you, Knebworth?"

Jack nodded.

"In fact, we all saw him," Mike went on, "and as I didn't like the idea of a coming star (if I may express that pious hope) being subjected to the annoyance of visiting monkeys, I sat up in the garden."

With a sudden impulsive gesture she put out her little hand, and Michael took it.

"Thank you, Mr Brixan," she said. "I have been wrong about you."

"Who isn't?" asked Mike with an extravagant shrug.

She returned to her room, and this time she closed her window. Once, before she went finally to sleep, she rose and, peeping through the curtains, saw the little glowing point of the watcher's cigar, and went back to bed comforted, to sleep as if it were only for a few minutes before Foss began knocking on the doors to waken the company.

The literary man himself was the first down. The garden was beginning to show palely in the dawn light, and he bade Michael Brixan a gruff good morning.

"Good morning to you," said Michael. "By the way, Mr Foss, you stayed behind at Griff Towers yesterday to see our friend Penne?"

"That's no business of yours," growled the man, and would have passed on, but Michael stood squarely in his path.

"There is one thing which is a business of mine, and that is to ask you why that little white disc appears on Miss Leamington's window?"

He pointed up to the white circle that the girl had seen the night before.

"I don't know anything about it," said Foss with rising anger, but there was also a note of fear in his voice.

"If you don't know, who will? Because I saw you put it there, just before it got dark last night."

"Well, if you must know," said the man, "it was to mark a vision boundary for the camera man."

That sounded a plausible excuse. Michael had seen Jack Knebworth marking out boundaries in the garden to ensure the actors being in the picture. At the first opportunity, when Knebworth appeared he questioned him on the subject.

"No, I gave no instructions to put up marks. Where is it?"

Michael showed him.

"I wouldn't have a mark up there, anyway, should I? Right in the middle of a window! What do you make of it?"

"I think Foss put it there with one object. The window was marked at Gregory's request."

"But why?" asked Knebworth, staring.

"To show Bhag Adele Leamington's room. That's why," said Michael, and he was confident that his view was an accurate one.

A CRY FROM A TOWER

Michael did not wait to see the early morning scenes shot. He had decided upon a course of action, and as soon as he conveniently could, he made his escape from the Dower House, and, crossing a field, reached the road which led to Griff Towers. Possessing a good eye for country, he had duly noted the field-path which ran along the boundary of Sir Gregory Penne's estate, and was, he guessed, a short cut to Griff; and ten minutes' walk brought him to the stile where the path joined the road. He walked quickly, his eyes on the ground, looking for some trace of the beast; but there had been no rain, and, unless he had wounded the animal, there was little hope that he would pick up the track.

Presently he came to the high flint wall which marked the southern end of the baronet's grounds, and this he followed until he came to a postern let in the wall, a door that appeared to have been recently in use, for it was ajar, he noted with satisfaction.

Pushing it open, he found himself in a large field which evidently served as kitchen garden for the house. There was nobody in sight. The grey tower looked even more forbidding and ugly in the early morning light. No smoke came from the chimneys; Griff was a house of the dead. Nevertheless, he proceeded cautiously, and, instead of crossing the field, moved back into the shadow of the wall until he reached the high boxwood fence that ran at right angles and separated the kitchen garden from that beautiful pleasaunce which Jack Knebworth had used the previous morning as a background for his scenes.

And all the time he kept his eyes roving, expecting at any moment to see the hideous figure of Bhag appear from the ground. At last he reached the end of the hedge. He was now within a few paces of the gravelled front, and less than half a dozen yards from the high, square grey tower which gave the house its name.

From where he stood he could see the whole front of the house. The drawn white blinds, the general lifelessness of Griff, might have convinced a less sceptical man than Mike Brixan that his suspicions were unfounded.

He was hesitating as to whether he should go to the house or not, when he heard a crash of glass, and looked up in time to see fragments falling from the topmost room of the tower. The sun had not yet risen, the earth was still wrapped in the illusory dawn light, and the hedge made an admirable hiding-place.

Who was breaking windows at this hour of the morning? Surely not the careful Bhag – so far he had reached in his speculations when the morning air was rent by a shrill scream, of such fear that his flesh went cold. It came from the upper room and ended abruptly, as though somebody had put his hand over the mouth of the unfortunate from whom that cry of terror had been wrung.

Hesitating no longer, Michael stepped from his place of concealment, ran quickly across the gravel, and pulled at the bell before the great entrance, which was immediately under the tower. He heard the clang of the bell and looked quickly round, to make absolutely sure that Bhag or some of the copper-coloured retainers of Griff Towers were not trailing him.

A minute passed – two – and his hand was again raised to the iron bell-pull, when he heard heavy feet in the corridor, a shuffle of slippers on the tiled floor of the hall, and a gruff voice demanded: "Who's there?"

"Michael Brixan."

There was a grunt, a rattle of chains, a snapping of locks, and the big door opened a few inches.

Gregory Penne was wearing a pair of grey flannel trousers and a shirt, the wristbands of which were unfastened. His malignant glare changed to wonder at the sight of the detective.

"What do you want?" he demanded, and opened the door a few more inches.

"I want to see you," said Michael.

"Usually call at daybreak?" growled the man as he closed the door on his visitor.

Michael made no answer, but followed Gregory Penne to his room. The library had evidently been occupied throughout the night. The windows were shuttered, the electroliers were burning, and before the fire was a table and two whisky bottles, one of which was empty.

"Have a drink?" said Penne mechanically, and poured himself out a portion with an unsteady hand.

"Is your ape in?" asked Michael, refusing the proffered drink with a gesture.

"What, Bhag? I suppose so. He goes and comes as he likes. Do you want to see him?"

"Not particularly," said Michael. "I've seen him once tonight."

Penne was lighting the stub of a cigar from the fire as he spoke, and he looked round quickly.

"You've seen him before? What do you mean?"

"I saw him at the Dower House, trying to get into Miss Leamington's room, and he was as near to being a dead orang-outang as he has ever been."

The man dropped the lighted spill on the hearth and stood up.

"Did you shoot him?" he asked.

"I shot at him."

Gregory nodded.

"You shot at him," he said softly. "That accounts for it. Why did you shoot him? He's perfectly harmless."

"He didn't strike me that way," said Michael coolly. "He was trying to pull Miss Leamington from her room."

The man's eyes opened.

"He got so far, did he? Well?"

There was a pause.

"You sent him to get the girl," said Michael. "You also bribed Foss to put a mark on the window so that Bhag should know where the girl was sleeping."

He paused, but the other made no reply.

"The cave man method is fairly beastly, even when the cave man does his own kidnapping. When he sends an anthropoid ape to do his dirty work, it passes into another category."

The man's eyes were invisible now; his face had grown a deeper hue.

"So that's your line, is it?" he said. "I thought you were a pal."

"I'm not responsible for your illusions," said Michael. "Only I tell you this" – he tapped the man's chest with his finger – "if any harm comes to Adele Leamington that is traceable to you or your infernal agent, I shan't be contented with shooting Mr Bhag; I will come here and shoot you! Do you understand? And now you can tell me, what is the meaning of that scream I heard from your tower?"

"Who the hell do you imagine you're cross-questioning?" spluttered Penne, livid with fury. "You dirty, miserable little actor!"

Michael slipped a card from his pocket and put it in the man's hand.

"You'll find my title to question you legibly inscribed," he said.

The man brought the card to the table-lamp and read it. The effect was electrical. His big jaw dropped, and the hand that held the card trembled so violently that it dropped to the floor.

"A detective?" he croaked. "A – a detective! What do you want here?"

"I heard somebody scream," said Michael.

"One of the servants, maybe. We've got a Papuan woman here who's ill: in fact, she's a little mad, and we're moving her tomorrow. I'll go and see if you like?"

He looked toward Michael as though seeking permission. His whole attitude was one of humility, and Michael required no more than the sight of that pallid face and those chattering teeth to turn his suspicion to certainty. Something was happening in this house that he must get to the bottom of.

"May I go and see?" asked Penne.

Michael nodded. The stout man shuffled out of the room as though he were in a hurry to be gone, and the lock clicked. Instantly Michael was at the door, turned the handle and pulled. It was locked!

He looked round the room quickly, and, running to one of the windows, flung back the curtain and pulled at the shutter. But this, too, was locked. It was, to all intents and purposes, a door with a little keyhole at the bottom. He was examining this when all the lights in the room went out, the only illumination being a faint red glow from the fire.

THE TRAP THAT FAILED

And then Michael heard a faint creak in one corner of the room. It was followed by the almost imperceptible sound of bare feet on the thick pile carpet, and the noise of quick breathing.

He did not hesitate. Feeling again for the keyhole of the shutter, he pulled out his pistol and fired twice at the lock. The sound of the explosion was deafening in the confined space of the room. It must have had an electrical effect upon the intruder, for when, with a wrench, the shutter opened, and at a touch the white blind sprang up, flooding with light the big, ornate room, it was empty.

Almost immediately afterwards the door opened through which the baronet had passed. If he had been panic-stricken before, his condition was now pitiable.

"What's that? What's that?" he whimpered. "Did somebody shoot?"

"Somebody shot," said Michael calmly, "and I was the somebody. And the gentlemen you sent into the room to settle accounts with me are very lucky that I confined my firing practice to the lock of your shutter, Penne."

He saw something white on the ground, and, crossing the room with quick strides, picked it up. It was a scarf of coarse silk, and he smelt it.

"Somebody dropped this in their hurry," he said. "I guess it was to be used."

"My dear fellow, I assure you I didn't know."

"How is the interesting invalid?" asked Michael with a curl of his lip. "The lunatic lady who screams?"

The man fingered his trembling lips for a moment as though he were trying to control them.

"She's all right. It was as I – as I thought," he said; "she had some sort of fit."

Michael eyed him pensively.

"I'd like to see her, if I may," he said.

"You can't." Penne's voice was loud, defiant. "You can't see anybody! What the hell do you mean by coming into my house at this hour of the morning and damaging my property? I'll have this matter reported to Scotland Yard, and I'll get the coat off your back, my man! Some of you detectives think you own the earth, but I'll show you you don't!"

The blustering voice rose to a roar. He was smothering his fear in weak anger, Michael thought, and looked up at the swords above the mantelpiece. Following the direction of his eyes, Sir Gregory wilted, and again his manner changed.

"My dear fellow, why exasperate me? I'm the nicest man in the world if you only treat me right. You've got crazy ideas about me, you have indeed!"

Michael did not argue. He walked slowly down the passage and out to meet the first sector of a blazing sun. As he reached the door he turned to the man.

"I cannot insist upon searching your house because I have not a warrant, as you know, and, by the time I'd got a warrant, there would be nothing to find. But you look out, my friend!" He waved a warning finger at the man. "I hate dragging in classical allusions, but I should advise you to look up a lady in mythology who was known to the Greeks as Adrastia!"

And with this he left, walking down the drive, watched with eyes of despair by a pale-faced girl from the upper window of the tower, whilst Sir Gregory went back to his library and, by much diligent searching, discovered that Adrastia was another name for Nemesis.

Michael was back at the Dower House in time for breakfast. It was no great tribute to his charm that his absence had passed unnoticed – or so it appeared, though Adele had marked his disappearance, and had been the first to note his return.

Jack Knebworth was in his most cheery mood. The scenes had been, he thought, most successful.

"I can't tell, of course, until I get back to the laboratory and develop the pictures; but so far as young Leamington is concerned, she's wonderful. I hate predicting at this early stage, but I believe that she's going to be a great artiste."

"You didn't expect her to be?" said Michael in surprise.

Jack laughed scornfully.

"I was very annoyed with Mendoza, and when I took this outfit on location, I did so quite expecting that I should have to return and retake the picture with Mendoza in the cast. Film stars aren't born, they're made; they're made by bitter experience, patience and suffering. They have got to pass through stages of stark inefficiency, during which they're liable to be discarded, before they win out. Your girl has skipped all the intervening phases, and has won at the first time of asking."

"When you talk about 'my girl,' " said Michael carefully, "will you be good enough to remember that I have the merest and most casual interest in the lady?"

"If you're not a liar," said Jack Knebworth, "you're a piece of cheese!"

"What chance has she as a film artiste?" asked Michael, anxious to turn the subject.

Knebworth ruffled his white hair. "Precious little," he said. "There isn't a chance for a girl in England. That's a horrible thing to say, but it's true. You can count the so-called English stars on the fingers of one hand; they've only a local reputation and they're generally married to the producer. What chance has an outsider got of breaking into the movies? And even if they break in, it's not much good to them. Production in this country is streets behind production either in America or in Germany. It is even behind the French, though the

French films are nearly the dullest in the world. The British producer has no ideas of his own; he can adopt and adapt the stunts, the tricks of acting, the methods of lighting, that he sees in foreign films at trade shows; and, with the aid of an American camera-man, he can produce something which might have been produced a couple of years ago at Hollywood. It's queer, because England has never been left behind as she has been in the cinema industry. France started the motorcar industry: today, England makes the finest motorcar in the world. America started aviation: today, the British aeroplanes have no superior. And yet, with all the example before them, with all the immense profits which are waiting to be made, in the past twenty years England has not produced one film star of international note, one film picture with an international reputation."

It was a subject upon which he was prepared to enlarge, and did enlarge, throughout the journey back to Chichester.

"The cinema industry is in the hands of showmen all the world over, but in England it is in the hands of peep-showmen, as against the Barnums of the States. No, there's no chance for your little friend, not in this country. If the picture I'm taking makes a hit in America – yes. She'll be playing at Hollywood in twelve months' time in an English story – directed by Americans!"

In the outer lobby of his office he found a visitor waiting for him, and gave her a curt and steely good morning.

"I want to see you, Mr Knebworth," said Stella Mendoza, with a smile at the leading man who had followed Knebworth into his office.

"You want to see me, do you? Why, you can see me now. What do you want?"

She was pulling at a lace handkerchief with a pretty air of penitence and confusion. Jack was not impressed. He himself had taught her all that handkerchief stuff.

"I've been very silly, Mr Knebworth, and I've come to ask your pardon. Of course, it was wrong to keep the boys and girls waiting, and I really am sorry. Shall I come in the morning? Or I can start today?"

A faint smile trembled at the corner of the director's big mouth.

"You needn't come in the morning and you needn't stay today, Stella," he said. "Your substitute has done remarkably well, and I don't feel inclined to retake the picture."

She flashed an angry glance at him, a glance at total variance with her softer attitude.

"I've got a contract: I suppose you know that, Mr Knebworth?" she said shrilly.

"I'd ever so much rather play opposite Miss Mendoza," murmured a gentle voice. It was the youthful Reggie Connolly, he of the sleek hair. "It's not easy to play opposite Miss — I don't even know her name. She's so – well, she lacks the artistry, Mr Knebworth."

Old Jack didn't speak. His gloomy eyes were fixed upon the youth.

"What's more, I don't feel I can do myself justice with Miss Mendoza out of the cast," said Reggie. "I really don't! I feel most awfully, terribly nervous, and it's difficult to express one's personality when one's awfully, terribly nervous. In fact," he said recklessly, "I'm not inclined to go on with the picture unless Miss Mendoza returns."

She shot a grateful glance at him, and then turned with a slow smile to the silent Jack.

"Would you like me to start today?"

"Not today, or any other day," roared the old director, his eyes flaming. "As for you, you nut-fed chorus boy, if you try to let me down I'll blacklist you at every studio in this country, and every time I meet you I'll kick you from hell to Halifax!"

He came stamping into the office, where Michael had preceded him, a raging fury of a man.

"What do you think of that?" he asked when he had calmed down. "That's the sort of stuff they try to get past you! He's going to quit in the middle of a picture! Did you hear him? That cissy-boy! That mouse! Say, Brixan, would you like to play opposite this girl of mine? You can't be worse than Connolly, and it would fill in your time whilst you're looking for the Head-Hunter."

Michael shook his head slowly.

"No, thank you," he said. "That is not my job. And as for the Head-Hunter" – he lit a cigarette and sent a ring of smoke to the ceiling – "I know who he is and I can lay my hands on him just when I want."

MENDOZA MAKES A FIGHT

Jack stared at him in amazement.

"You're joking!" he said.

"On the contrary, I am very much in earnest," said Michael quietly. "But to know the Head-Hunter, and to bring his crimes home to him, are quite different matters."

Jack Knebworth sat at his desk, his hands thrust into his trousers pockets, a look of blank incredulity on the face turned to the detective.

"Is it one of my company?" he asked, troubled, and Michael laughed.

"I haven't the pleasure of knowing all your company," he said diplomatically, "but at any rate, don't let the Head-Hunter worry you. What are you going to do about Mr Reggie Connolly?"

The director shrugged.

"He doesn't mean it, and I was a fool to get wild," he said. "That kind of ninny never means anything. You wouldn't dream, to see him on the screen, full of tenderness and love and manliness, that he's the poor little jellyfish he is! As for Mendoza – " he swept his hands before him, and the gesture was significant.

Miss Stella Mendoza, however, was not accepting her dismissal so readily. She had fought her way up from nothing, and was not prepared to forfeit her position without a struggle. Moreover, her position was a serious one. She had money – so much money that she need never work again; for, in addition to her big salary, she enjoyed an income from a source which need not be too closely inquired into.

But there was a danger that Knebworth might carry the war into a wider field.

Her first move was to go in search of Adele Leamington, who, she learnt that morning for the first time, had taken her place. Though she went in a spirit of conciliation, she choked with anger to discover that the girl was occupying the star's dressing-room, the room which had always been sacred to Stella Mendoza's use. Infuriated, yet preserving an outward calm, she knocked at the door. (That she, Stella Mendoza, should knock at a door rightfully hers was maddening enough!)

Adele was sitting at the bare dressing-table, gazing, a little awestricken, at the array of mirrors, lights and the vista of dresses down the long alleyway which served as a wardrobe. At the sight of Mendoza she went red.

"Miss Leamington, isn't it?" asked Stella sweetly. "May I come in?"

"Do, please," said Adele, hastily rising.

"Please *do* sit down," said Stella. "It's a very uncomfortable chair, but most of the chairs here are uncomfortable. They tell me you have been 'doubling' for me?"

" 'Doubling'?" said Adele, puzzled.

"Yes, Mr Knebworth said he was 'doubling' you. You know what I mean: when an artiste can't appear, they sometimes put in an understudy in scenes where she's not very distinctly shown – long shots – "

"But Mr Knebworth took me close up," said the girl quietly. "I was only in one long shot."

Miss Mendoza masked her anger and sighed. "Poor old chap! He's very angry with me, and really, I oughtn't to annoy him. I'm coming back tomorrow, you know."

The girl went pale.

"It's fearfully humiliating for you, I realize, but, my dear, we've all had to go through that experience. And people in the studio will be very nice to you."

"But it's impossible," said Adele. "Mr Knebworth told me I was to be in the picture from start to finish."

Mendoza shook her head smilingly.

"You can never believe what these fellows tell you," she said. "He's just told me to be ready to shoot tomorrow morning on the South Downs."

Adele's heart sank. She knew that was the rendezvous, though she was not aware of the fact that Stella Mendoza had procured her information from the disgruntled Mr Connolly.

"It *is* humiliating," Stella went on thoughtfully. "If I were you, I would go up to town and stay away for a couple of weeks till the whole thing has blown over. I feel very much to blame for your disappointment, my dear, and if money is any compensation – " She opened her bag and, taking out a wad of notes, detached four and put them on the table.

"What is this for?" asked Adele coldly.

"Well, my dear, you'll want money for expenses – "

"If you imagine I'm going to London without seeing Mr Knebworth and finding out for myself whether you're speaking the truth – "

Mendoza's face flamed.

"Do you suggest I'm lying?"

She had dropped all pretence of friendliness and stood, a veritable virago, her hands on her hips, her dark face thrust down into Adele's.

"I don't know whether you're a liar or whether you are mistaken," said Adele, who was less afraid of this termagant than she had been at the news she had brought. "The only thing I'm perfectly certain about is that for the moment this is my room, and I will ask you to leave it!"

She opened the door, and for a moment was afraid that the girl would strike her; but the broad-shouldered Irish dresser, a silent but passionately interested spectator and audience, interposed her huge bulk and good-humouredly pushed the raging star into the corridor.

"I'll have you out of there!" she screamed across the woman's shoulder. "Jack Knebworth isn't everything in this company! I've got influence enough to fire Knebworth!"

The unrepeatable innuendoes that followed were not good to hear, but Adele Leamington listened in scornful silence. She was only too relieved (for the girl's fury was eloquent) to know that she had not been speaking the truth. For one horrible moment Adele had believed her, knowing that Knebworth would not hesitate to sacrifice her or any other member of the company if, by so doing, the values of the picture could be strengthened.

Knebworth was alone when his ex-star was announced, and his first instinct was not to see her. Whatever his intentions might have been, she determined his action by appearing in the doorway just as he was making up his mind what line to take. He fixed her with his gimlet eyes for a second, and then, with a jerk of his head, called her in. When they were alone: "There are many things I admire about you. Stella, and not the least of them is your nerve. But it is no good coming to me with any of that let-bygones-be-bygones stuff. You're not appearing in this picture, and maybe you'll never appear in another picture of mine."

"Is that so?" she drawled, sitting down uninvited, and taking from her bag a little gold cigarette case.

"You've come in to tell me that you've got influence with a number of people who are financially interested in this corporation," said Jack, to her dismay. She wondered if there were telephone communication between the dressing-room and the office, then remembered there wasn't.

"I've handled a good many women in my time," he went on, "and I've never had to fire one but she didn't produce the President, Vice-President or Treasurer and hold them over my head with their feet ready to kick out my brains! And, Stella, none of those hold-ups have ever got past. People who are financially interested in a company may love you to death, but they've got to have the money to love you with; and if I don't make pictures that sell, somebody is short of a perfectly good diamond necklace."

"We'll see if Sir Gregory thinks the same way," she said defiantly, and Jack Knebworth whistled.

"Gregory Penne, eh? I didn't know you had friends in that quarter. Yes, he is a stockholder in the company, but he doesn't hold enough to make any difference. I guess he told you that he did. And if he held ninety-nine per cent of it, Stella, it wouldn't make any difference to old Jack Knebworth, because old Jack Knebworth's got a contract which gives him carte blanche, and the only getting out clause is the one that gets *me* out! You couldn't touch me, Stella, no, ma'am!"

"I suppose you're going to blacklist me?" she said sulkily.

This was the one punishment she most feared — that Jack Knebworth should circulate the story of her unforgivable sin of letting down a picture when it was half-shot.

"I thought about that," he nodded, "but I guess I'm not vindictive. I'll let you go and say the part didn't suit you, and that you resigned, which is as near the truth as any story I'll have to crack. Go with God, Stella. I guess you won't, because you're not that way, but — behave!"

He waved her out of the office and she went, somewhat chastened. Outside the studio she met Lawley Foss, and told him the result of the interview.

"If it's like that you can do nothing," he said. "I'd speak for you, Stella, but I've got to speak for myself," he added bitterly. "The idea of a man of my genius truckling hat in hand to this damned old Yankee is very humiliating."

"You ought to have your own company, Lawley," she said, as she had said a dozen times before. "You write the stuff and I'll be the leading woman and put it over for you. Why, you could direct Kneb's head off. I *know*, Lawley! I've been to the only place on God Almighty's earth where art is appreciated, and I tell you that a four-flusher like Jack Knebworth wouldn't last a light-mile at Hollywood!"

"Light-mile" was a term she had acquired from a scientific admirer. It had the double advantage of sounding grand and creating a demand for an explanation. To her annoyance, Foss was sufficiently acquainted with elementary physics to know that she meant the period of time that a ray of light would take to traverse a mile.

"Is he in his office now?"

She nodded, and without any further word Lawley Foss, in some trepidation, knocked at his chief's door.

"The truth is, Mr Knebworth, I want to ask a favour of you."

"Is it money?" demanded Jack, looking up from under his bushy brows.

"Well, it was money, as a matter of fact. There have been one or two little bills I've overlooked, and the bailiffs have been after me. I've got to raise fifty pounds by two o'clock this afternoon."

Jack pulled open a drawer, took out a book and wrote a cheque, not for fifty pounds, but for eighty.

"That's a month's salary in advance," he said. "You've drawn your pay up to today, and by the terms of your contract you're entitled to one month's notice or pay therefore. You've got it."

Foss went an ugly red.

"Does that mean I'm fired?" he asked loudly.

Jack nodded.

"You're fired, not because you want money, not because you're one of the most difficult men on the lot to deal with, but for what you did last night, Foss."

"What do you mean?"

"I mean I am taking Mr Brixan's view, that you fastened a white label to the window of Miss Leamington's room in order to guide an agent of Sir Gregory Penne. That agent came and nearly kidnapped my leading lady."

The man's lip curled in a sneer.

"You've got melodrama in your blood, Knebworth," he said. "Kidnap your leading lady! Those sort of things may happen in the United States, but they don't happen in England."

"Close the door as you go out," said Jack, preparing for his work.

"Let me say this – " began Foss.

"I'll let you say nothing," snarled Knebworth. "I won't even let you say 'goodbye.' Get!"

And, when the door slammed behind his visitor, the old director pushed a bell on his table, and, to his assistant who came: "Get Miss Leamington down here," he said. "I'd like contact with something that's wholesome."

TWO FROM THE YARD

Chichester is not famous for its restaurants, but the dining-room of a little hotel, where three people foregathered that afternoon, had the advantage of privacy.

When Mike Brixan got back to his hotel he found two men waiting to see him, and, after a brief introduction, he took them upstairs to his sitting-room.

"I'm glad you've come," he said, when the inspector had closed the door behind him. "The fact is that sheerly criminal work is a novelty to me, and I'm afraid that I'm going to make it a mystery to you," he smiled. "At the moment I'm not prepared to give expression to all my suspicions."

Detective Inspector Lyle, the chief of the two, laughed.

"We have been placed entirely under your orders, Captain Brixan," he said, "and neither of us are very curious. The information you asked for, Sergeant Walters has brought." He indicated his tall companion.

"Which information – about Penne? Is he known to the police?" asked Michael, interested.

Sergeant Walters nodded.

"He was convicted and fined a few years ago for assaulting a servant – a woman. Apparently he took a whip to the girl, and he very narrowly escaped going to prison. That was the first time our attention was attracted to him, and we made inquiries both in London and in the Malay States and found out all about him. He's a very rich man, and, being a distant cousin of the late baronet, you may say he fluked his title. In Borneo he lived up-country, practically in the bush, for fifteen or twenty years, and the stories we have about him aren't particularly savoury. There are a few of them which you might read at your leisure, Mr Brixan – they're in the record."

Michael nodded.

"Is anything known of an educated orang-outang which is his companion?"

To his surprise, the officer answered: "Bhag? Oh yes, we know all about him. He was captured when he was quite a baby by Penne, and was brought up in captivity. It has been rather difficult to trace the man, because he never returns to England by the usual steamship line, so that it's almost impossible to have a tag on him. He has a yacht, a fine sea-going boat, the *Kipi*, which is practically officered and manned by Papuans. What comes and goes with him I don't know. There was a complaint came through to us that the last time he was abroad Penne nearly lost his life as the result of some quarrel he had with a local tribesman. Now, Mr Brixan, what would you like us to do?"

Michael's instructions were few and brief. That evening, when Adele walked home to her lodgings, she was conscious that a man was following her, and after her previous night's adventure this fact would have played havoc with her nerves but for the note she found waiting when she got indoors. It was from Michael.

Would you mind if I put a Scotland Yard man to watch you, to see that you do not get into mischief! I don't think there's any danger that you will, but I shall feel ever so much easier in my mind if you will endure this annoyance.

She read the letter and her brows knit. So she was being shadowed! It was an uncomfortable experience, and yet she could not very well object, could not indeed feel anything but a sense of warm gratitude toward this ubiquitous and pushful young man, who seemed determined not to let her out of his sight.

THE BROWN MAN FROM NOWHERE

With a brand-new grievance against life, Lawley Foss gathered his forces to avenge himself upon the world that had treated him so harshly. And first and most powerful of his forces was Stella Mendoza. There was a council of war held in the drawing-room of the pretty little house that Stella had taken when she joined the Knebworth Corporation. The third of the party was Mr Reggie Connolly. And as they were mutually sympathetic, so were they mutually unselfish – characteristically so.

"We've been treated disgracefully by Knebworth, Mr Foss, especially you. I think, compared with your case, mine is nothing."

"It is the way he has handled you that makes me sore," said Foss energetically. "An artiste of your standing!"

"The work you've done for him. And Reggie – he treated him like a dog!"

"Personally, it doesn't matter to me," said Reggie. "I can always find a contract – it's you – "

"For the matter of that, we can *all* find contracts," interrupted Stella with a taste of acid in her voice; "I can have my own company when I please, and I've got two directors mad to direct me, and two men I know would put up every cent of money to give me my own company – at least, they'd put up a lot. And Chauncey Seller is raving to play opposite me, and you know what a star he is; and he'd let me be featured and go into small type himself. He's a lovely man, and the best juvenile in this country or any other."

Mr Connolly coughed.

"The point is, can we get the money *now*?" asked Foss, practical for once.

There was no immediate and enthusiastic assurance from the girl.

"Because, if not, I think I can get all I want," said Foss surprisingly. "I won't say from whom, or how I'm going to get it. But I'm certain I can get big money, and it will be easier to get it for some specific object than to ask for it for myself."

"Less risky?" suggested Connolly, with a desire to be in the conversation.

It was an unfortunate remark, the more so since by chance he had hit the nail on the head. Foss went a dull red.

"What the hell do you mean by 'less risky'?" he demanded.

Poor Reggie had meant nothing, and admitted as much in some haste. He had meant to be helpful, and was ready to sulk at the storm he had aroused. More ready because, as the conversation had progressed, he had faded more and more into the background as an inconsiderable factor. There is nothing quite so disheartening to a conspirator as to find the conspiring taken out of his hands, and Reggie Connolly felt it was the moment to make a complete *volte face*, and incidentally assert what he was pleased to call his "personality."

"This is all very well, Stella," he said, "but it looks to me as if I'm going to be left out in the cold. What with your thinking about Chauncey Seller – he's let down more pictures than any two men I know – and all that sort of thing, I don't see that I'm going to be much use to you. I don't really. I know you'll think I'm a fearful, awful rotter, but I feel that we owe something to old Jack Kneb, I do really. I've jeopardized my position for your sake, and I'm prepared to do anything in reason, but what with pulling Chauncey Seller – who is a bounder of the worst kind – into your cast, and what with Foss jumping down my throat, well, really – really!"

They were not inclined to mollify him, having rather an eye to the future than to the present, and he had retired in a huff before the girl realized that the holding of Reggie would at least have embarrassed Knebworth to the extent of forcing a retake of those parts of the picture in which he appeared.

"Never mind about Connolly. The picture is certain to fail with that extra: she's bad. I have a friend in London," explained Foss, after the discussion returned to the question of ways and means, "who can put up the money. I've got a sort of pull with him. In fact – well, anyhow – I've got a pull. I'll go up tonight and see him."

"And I'll see mine," said Stella. "We'll call the company The Stella Mendoza Picture Corporation – "

Lawley Foss demurred. He was inclined to another title, and was prepared to accept as a compromise the Foss-Mendoza or F M Company, a compromise agreeable to Stella provided the initials were reversed.

"Who is Brixan?" she asked as Foss was leaving.

"He is a detective."

She opened her eyes wide.

"A detective? Whatever is he doing here?"

Lawley Foss smiled contemptuously.

"He is trying to discover what no man of his mental calibre will ever discover, the Head-Hunter. I am the one man in the world who could help him. Instead of which," he smiled again, "I am helping myself."

With which cryptic and mystifying statement he left her.

Stella Mendoza was an ambitious woman, and when ambition is directed toward wealth and fame it is not attended by scruple. Her private life and her standard of values were no better and no worse than thousands of other women, and no more belonged to her profession than did her passion for good food and luxurious environment. The sins of any particular class or profession are not peculiar to their status or calling, but to their self-education in the matter of the permissible. As one woman would die rather than surrender her self-respect, so another would lose her self-respect rather than suffer poverty and hardship, and think little or nothing of the act or the deceit she practised to gain her ends.

After Foss had gone, she went up to her room to change. It was too early to make the call she intended, for Sir Gregory did not like to see her during the daytime. He, who had not hesitated to send Bhag on a fantastic mission, was a stickler for the proprieties.

Having some letters to post, she drove into Chichester late in the afternoon, and saw Mike Brixan in peculiar circumstances. He was the centre of a little crowd near the market cross, a head above the surrounding people. There was a policeman present: she saw his helmet, and for a moment was inclined to satisfy her curiosity. She changed her mind, and when she returned the crowd had dispersed and Michael had disappeared, and driving home, she wondered whether the detective had been engaged professionally.

Mike himself had been attracted by the crowd which was watching the ineffectual efforts of a Sussex policeman to make himself intelligible to a shock-haired, brown-faced native, an incongruous figure in an ill-fitting suit of store clothes and a derby hat which was a little too large for him. In his hand he carried a bundle tied up in a bright green handkerchief, and under his arm a long object, wrapped in linen and fastened with innumerable strings. At the first sight of him Michael thought it was one of Penne's Malayan servants, but on second thoughts he realized that Sir Gregory would not allow any of his slaves to run loose about the countryside.

Pushing his way through the crowd, he came up to the policeman, who touched his helmet rim and grinned.

"Can't make head or tail of this fellow's lingo, sir," he said. "He wants to know something, but I can't make out what. He has just come into the city."

The brown man turned his big dark eyes upon Mike and said something which was Greek to the detective. There was a curious dignity about the native that even his ludicrous garments could not wholly dissipate, an erectness of body, a carriage of head, an imponderable air of greatness that instantly claimed Michael Brixan's attention.

Then suddenly he had an inspiration, and addressed the man in Dutch. Immediately the native's eyes lit up.

"*Ja, mynheer*, I speak Dutch."

Mike had guessed that he came from Malaya, where Dutch and Portuguese are spoken by the better class natives.

"I am from Borneo, and I seek a man who is called Truji, an Englishman. No, *mynheer*, I wish to see his house, for he is a great man in my country. When I have seen his house I will go back to Borneo."

Mike was watching him as he talked. It was a particularly good-looking face, except for the long and ugly scar that ran from his forehead to the point of his jaw.

A new servant for Gregory Penne, thought the detective, and gave him directions. Standing by the policeman's side, he watched the queer figure with its bundles till it disappeared.

"Queer language, that, sir," said the officer. "It was Dutch to me."

"And to me," chuckled Mike, and continued his way to the hotel.

MR FOSS MAKES A SUGGESTION

Immersed in her beloved script, Adele Leamington sat on her bed, a box of *marron glacé* by her side, her knees tucked up, and a prodigious frown on her forehead. Try as hard as she would, she found it impossible to concentrate upon the intricate directions with which Foss invariably tortured the pages of his scenarios. Ordinarily she could have mastered this handicap, but, for some reason or other, individual thoughts which belonged wholly to her and had no association with her art came flowing forth in such volume that the lines were meaningless and the page, for all the instruction it gave to her, might as well have been blank.

What *was* Michael Brixan? He was not her idea of a detective, and why was he staying in Chichester? Could it be…? She flushed at the thought and was angry with herself. It was hardly likely that a man who was engaged in unravelling a terrible crime would linger for the sake of being near to her. Was the Head-Hunter, the murderer, living near Chichester? She dropped her manuscript to her knees at the appalling thought.

The voice of her landlady aroused her.

"Will you see Mr Foss, miss?"

She jumped up from the bed and opened the door.

"Where is he?"

"I've put him in the parlour," said the woman, who had grown a little more respectful of late. Possibly the rise of the extra to stardom was generally known in that small town, which took an interest in the fortunes of its one ewe lamb of a production company.

Lawley Foss was standing by the window, looking out, when she came into the room.

"Good afternoon, Adele," he said genially. (He had never called her by her Christian name before, even if he had known it.)

"Good afternoon, Mr Foss," she said with a smile. "I'm sorry to hear that you have left us."

Foss lifted his shoulders in a gesture of indifference.

"The scope was a little too limited for my kind of work," he said.

He was wondering if Mike had told her about the disc of paper on her window, and surmised rightly that he had not. Foss himself did not attach any significance to the white disc, accepting Gregory's explanation, which was that, liking the girl, he wished to toss some flowers and a present, by way of a peace offering, through a window which he guessed would be open. Foss had thought him a love-sick fool, and had obliged him. The story that Knebworth had told he dismissed as sheer melodrama.

"Adele, you're a foolish little girl to turn down a man like Gregory Penne," he said, and saw by her face that he was on dangerous ground. "There's no sense in getting up in the air; after all, we're human beings, and it isn't unnatural that Penne should have a crush on you. There's nothing wrong in that. Hundreds of girls have dinner with men without there being anything sinister in it. I'm a friend of Penne's, in a way, and I'm seeing him tonight on a very important and personal matter – will you come along?"

She shook her head.

"There may be no harm in it," she said, "but there is no pleasure in it either."

"He's a rich man and a powerful man," said Foss impressively. "He could be of service to you."

Again she shook her head.

"I want no other help than my own ability," she said. "I nearly said 'genius,' but that would have sounded like conceit. I do not need the patronage of any rich man. If I cannot succeed without that, then I am a hopeless failure and am content to be one!"

Still Foss lingered.

"I think I can manage without you," he said, "but I'd have been glad of your co-operation. He's crazy about you. If Mendoza knew that, she'd kill you!"

"Miss Mendoza?" gasped the girl. "But why? Does she – she know him?"

He nodded.

"Yes: very few people are aware of the fact. There was a time when he'd have done anything for her, and she was a wise girl: she let him help! Mendoza has money to burn and diamonds enough to fill the Jewel House."

Adele listened, horror-stricken, incredulous, and he hastened to insure himself against Stella's wrath.

"You needn't tell her I told you – this is in strict confidence. I don't want to get on the wrong side of Penne either," he shivered. "That man's a devil!"

Her lips twitched.

"And yet you calmly ask me to dine with him, and hold out the bait of Miss Mendoza's diamonds!"

"I suppose you think she's awful," he sneered.

"I am very sorry for her," said the girl quietly, "and I am determined not to be sorry for myself!"

She opened the door to him in silence, and in silence he took his departure. After all, he thought, there was no need for any outside help. In his breast pocket was a sheet of manuscript, written on the Head-Hunter's typewriter. That ought to be worth thousands when he made his revelation.

THE FACE IN THE PICTURE

Mr Sampson Longvale was taking a gentle constitutional on the strip of path before his untidy house. He wore, as usual – for he was a creature of habit – a long, grey silk dressing-gown, fastened by a scarlet sash. On his head was his silk nightcap, and between his teeth a clay churchwarden pipe, which he puffed solemnly as he walked.

He had just bidden a courteous good night to the help who came in daily to tidy his living-rooms and prepare his simple meals, when he heard the sound of feet coming up the drive. He thought at first it was the woman returning (she had a habit of forgetting things); but when he turned, he saw the unprepossessing figure of a neighbour with whom he was acquainted in the sense that Sir Gregory Penne had twice been abominably rude to him.

The old man watched with immobile countenance the coming of his unwelcome visitor.

"Evening!" growled Penne. "Can I speak to you privately?"

Mr Longvale inclined his head courteously.

"Certainly, Sir Gregory. Will you come in?"

He ushered the owner of Griff Towers into the long sitting-room and lit the candles. Sir Gregory glanced round, his lips curled in disgust at the worn poverty of the apartment, and when the old man had pushed up a chair for him, it was some time before he accepted the offer.

"Now, sir," said Mr Longvale courteously, "to what circumstances do I owe the pleasure of this visit?"

"You had some actors staying here the other day?"

Mr Longvale inclined his head.

"There was some fool talk about a monkey of mine trying to get into the house."

"A monkey?" said Mr Longvale in gentle surprise. "That is the first I have heard of monkeys."

Which was true. The other looked at him suspiciously.

"Is that so?" he asked. "You're not going to persuade me you didn't hear?"

The old man stood up, a picture of dignity.

"Do you suggest that I am lying, sir?" he said. "Because, if you do, there is the door! And though it hurts me to be in the least degree discourteous to a guest of mine, I am afraid I have no other course than to ask you to leave my house."

"All right, all right," said Sir Gregory Penne impatiently. "Don't lose your temper, my friend. I didn't come to see you about that, anyway. You're a doctor, aren't you?"

Mr Longvale was obviously startled.

"I practised medicine when I was younger," he said.

"Poor, too?" Gregory looked round "You haven't a shilling in the world, I'll bet!"

"There you are wrong," said old Mr Longvale quietly. "I am an extremely wealthy man, and the fact that I do not keep my house in repair is due to the curious penchant of mine for decaying things. That is an unhealthy, probably a morbid predilection of mine. How did you know I was a doctor?"

"I heard through one of my servants. You set the broken finger of a carter."

"I haven't practised for years," said Mr Longvale. "I almost wish I had," he added wistfully. "It is a noble science – "

"Anyway," interrupted Penne, "even if you can't be bought, you're a secretive old devil, and that suits me. There's a girl up at my house who is very ill. I don't want any of these prying country doctors nosing around my private affairs. Would you come along and see her?"

The old man pursed his lips thoughtfully.

"I should be most happy," he said, "but I am afraid my medical science is a little rusty. Is she a servant?"

"In a way," said the other shortly. "When can you come?"

"I'll come at once," said Mr Longvale gravely, and went out, to return in his greatcoat.

The baronet looked at the ancient garment with a smile of derision.

"Why the devil do you wear such old-fashioned clothes?" he asked.

"To me they are very new," said the old man gently. "The garments of today are without romance, without the thrill which these bring to me." He patted the overlapping cape and smiled. "An old man is entitled to his fancies: let me be humoured, Sir Gregory."

At the moment Mr Sampson Longvale was driving to Griff Towers, Mike Brixan, summoned by messenger, was facing Jack Knebworth in his office.

"I hope you didn't mind my sending for you, though it was a fool thing to do," said the director. "You remember that we shot some scenes at Griff Towers?"

Michael nodded.

"I want you to see one that we took, with the tower in the background, and tell me what you think of – something."

Wonderingly, Michael accompanied the director to the projection room.

"My laboratory manager pointed it out to me in the negative," explained Jack as they seated themselves and the room went dark. "Of course, I should have seen it in the print."

"What is it?" asked Michael curiously.

"That's just what I don't know," said the other, scratching his head, "but you'll see for yourself."

There was a flicker and a furious clicking, and there appeared on the small screen which was used for projection purposes, a picture of two people. Adele was one and Reggie Connolly the other, and Michael gazed stolidly, though with rising annoyance, at a love scene which was being enacted between the two.

In the immediate background was the wall of the tower, and Michael saw for the first time that there was a little window which he did not remember having seen from the interior of the hall; it was particularly dark, and was lighted, even in daytime, by electric lamps.

"I never noticed that window before," he said.

"It's the window I want you to watch," said Jack Knebworth, and, even as he spoke, there came stealthily into view a face.

At first it was indistinct and blurred, but later, it came into focus. It was the oval face of a girl, dark-eyed, her hair in disorder, a look of unspeakable terror on her face. She raised her hand as if to beckon somebody – probably Jack himself, who was directing the picture. That, at least, was Jack's view. They had hardly time to get accustomed to the presence of the mystery girl when she disappeared, with such rapidity as to suggest that she had been dragged violently back.

"What do you make of that?" asked Knebworth.

Michael bit his lip thoughtfully.

"Looks almost as though friend Penne had a prisoner in his dark tower. Of course, the woman whose scream I heard, and who he said was a servant! But the window puzzles me. There's no sign of it inside. The stairway leads out of the hall, but in such a position that it is impossible that the girl could have been standing either on the stairs or the landing. Therefore, there must be a fifth wall inside, containing a separate staircase. Does this mean you will have to retake?"

Jack shook his head.

"No, we can back her out: she's only on fifty feet of the film; but I thought you'd like to see it."

The lights came on again, and they went back to the director's office.

"I don't like Penne, for more reasons than one," said Jack Knebworth. "I like him less since I've found that he's better friends with Mendoza than I thought he was."

"Who is Mendoza – the deposed star?"

The other nodded.

"Stella Mendoza – not a bad girl and not a good girl," he said. "I've been wondering why Penne always gave us permission to use his grounds for shooting, and now I know. I tell you that that house holds a few secrets!"

Michael smiled faintly.

"One, at least, of them will be revealed tonight," he said. "I am going to explore Griff Towers, and I do not intend asking permission of Sir Gregory Penne. And if I can discover, what I believe is there to be discovered, Gregory Penne will sleep under lock and key this night!"

THE MIDNIGHT VISIT

Michael Brixan had had sent down to him from town a heavy suitcase, which contained precious little clothing. He was busy with its contents for half an hour, when the boots of the hotel announced the arrival of the motorcycle that had been hired for him.

With a canvas bag strapped to his back, he mounted the machine, and was soon clear of the town, swerving through the twisting lanes of Sussex until he arrived at the Dower House, behind which he concealed his machine.

It was eleven o'clock when he crossed the fields to the postern gate, on the alert all the time for the soft-footed Bhag. The postern was closed and locked – a contingency for which he was prepared. Unstrapping his bag, he took therefrom a bundle of rods, and screwed three together. To the top he fastened a big, blunt hook, and, replacing the remainder of the rods, he lifted the hook till it rested on the top of the high wall, tested its stability, and in a few seconds had climbed his "ladder" and had jumped to the other side.

He followed the path that he had taken before, keeping close to the bushes, and all the time watching left and right for Penne's monstrous servant. As he came to the end of the hedge, the hall door opened and two men came out. One was Penne, and for a moment he did not recognize the tall man by his side, until he heard his voice. Mr Sampson Longvale!

"I think she will be all right. The wounds are very peculiar. It looks almost as if she had been scratched by some huge claw," said Longvale.

"I hope I have been of assistance, Sir Gregory, though, as I told you, it is nearly fifty years since I engaged in medical work."

So old Longvale had been a doctor! Somehow this news did not surprise Michael. There was something in the old man's benevolence of countenance and easy manner which would have suggested a training in that profession, to one less analytical than Michael Brixan.

"My car will take you down," he heard Sir Gregory say.

"No, no, thank you; I will walk. It is not very far. Good night, Sir Gregory."

The baronet growled a good night and went back into the dimly-lit hall, and Michael heard the rattle of chains as the door was fastened.

There was no time to be lost. Almost before Mr Sampson Longvale had disappeared into the darkness, Michael had opened his canvas bag and had screwed on three more links to his ladder. From each rod projected a short, light, steel bracket. It was the type of hook-ladder that firemen use, and Michael had employed this method of gaining entrance to a forbidden house many times in his chequered career.

He judged the distance accurately, for when he lifted the rod and dropped the hook upon the sill of the little window, the ladder hung only a few inches short of the ground. With a tug to test the hook, he went up hand over hand, and in a few seconds was prying at the window sash. It needed little opening, for the catch was of elementary simplicity, and in another instant he was standing on the step of a dark and narrow stairway.

He had provided himself with an electric torch, and he flashed a beam up and down. Below, he saw a small door which apparently led into the hall, and, by an effort of memory, he remembered that in the corner of the hall he had seen a curtain hanging, without attaching any importance to the fact. Going down, he tried the door and found it locked. Putting down his lantern, he took out a leather case of tools and began to manipulate the lock. In an incredibly short space of time the key turned. When he had assured himself that the door would open, he was satisfied. For the moment his work lay upstairs, and he climbed the steps again, coming to a narrow landing, but no door.

A second, a third and a fourth flight brought him, as near as he could guess, to the top of the tower, and here he found a narrow exit. Listening, after a while he heard somebody moving about the room, and by the sound they made, he supposed they wore slippers. Presently a door closed with a thud, and he tried the handle of the wicket. It was unlocked, and he opened it gently a fraction of an inch at a time, until he secured a view of the greater part of the chamber.

It was a small, lofty room, unfurnished with the exception of a low bed in one corner, on which a woman lay. Her back was toward him, fortunately; but the black hair and the ivory yellow of the bare arm that lay on the coverlet told him that she was not European.

Presently she turned and he saw her face, recognizing her immediately as the woman whose face he had seen in the picture. She was pretty in her wild way, and young. Her eyes were closed, and presently she began crying softly in her sleep.

Michael was halfway in the room when he saw the handle of the other door turn, and, quick as a flash, stepped back into the darkness of the landing.

It was Bhag, in his old blue overall, a tray of food in his great hands. He reached out his foot and pulled the table toward him, placing the viands by the side of the bed. The girl opened her eyes and sank back with a little cry of disgust; and Bhag, who was evidently used to these demonstrations of her loathing, shuffled out of the room.

Again Michael pushed the door and crossed the room, unnoticed by the girl, looking out into the passage – not six feet away from him, Bhag was squatting, glaring in his direction.

Michael closed the door quickly and flew back to the secret staircase, pulling the door behind him. He felt for a key, but there was none, and, without wasting another second, he ran down the stairs. The one thing he wished to avoid was an encounter which would betray his presence in the house.

He made no attempt to get out of the window, but continued his way to the foot of the stairs, and passed through into the hall. This time he was able to close the door, for there were two large bolts at the top and the bottom. Pulling aside the curtain, he stepped gingerly into the hall. For a while he waited, and presently heard the shuffle of feet on the stairs and a sniff beneath the door.

His first act was to ensure his retreat. Noiselessly he drew the bolts from the front door, slipped off the chain and turned the key. Then, as noiselessly, he made his way along the corridor toward Sir Gregory's room.

The danger was that one of the native servants would see him, but this he must risk. He had observed on each of his previous visits that, short of the library, a door opened into what he knew must be an ante-room of some kind. It was unlocked and he stepped into complete darkness. Groping along the wall, he found a row of switches, and pulled down the first. This lit two wall-brackets, sufficient to give him a general view of the apartment.

It was a small drawing-room, apparently unused, for the furniture was sheeted with nolland, and the fire-grate was empty. From here it was possible to gain access to the library through a door near the window. He switched off the light, locked the door on the inside, and tried the shutters. These were fastened by iron bars and were not, as in the case of the library, locked. He pulled them back, let the blind up, and gingerly raised a window. His second line of retreat was now prepared, and he could afford to take risks.

Kneeling down, he looked through the keyhole. The library was illuminated, and somebody was talking. A woman! Turning the handle, he opened the door the fraction of an inch, and had a view of the interior.

Gregory Penne was standing in his favourite attitude, with his back to the fire, and before him was a tray of those refreshments without which life was apparently insupportable. Seated on the low settee, drawn up at one side of the fireplace, was Stella Mendoza. She was wearing a fur coat, for the night was chilly, and about her neck was such a sparkle of gems as Michael had never seen before on a woman.

Evidently the discussion was not a pleasant one, for there was a heavy scowl on Gregory's face, and Stella did not seem too pleased.

"I left you because I had to leave you," growled the man, answering some complaint she had made. "One of my servants is ill and I brought in the doctor. And if I had stayed it would have been the same. It's no good, my girl," he said harshly. "The goose doesn't lay golden eggs more than once – this goose doesn't, at any rate. You were a fool to quarrel with Knebworth."

She said something which did not reach Michael's ears.

"I dare say your own company would be fine," said Penne sarcastically. "It would be fine for me, who footed the bill, and finer for you, who spent the money! No! Stella, that cat doesn't jump. I've been very good to you, and you've no right to expect me to bankrupt myself to humour your whims."

"It's not a whim," she said vehemently, "it's a necessity. You don't want to see me going round the studios taking any kind of job I can get, do you, Gregory?" she pleaded.

"I don't want to see you work at all, and there's no reason why you should. You've enough to live on. Anyway, you've got nothing against Knebworth. If it hadn't been for him, you wouldn't have met me, and if you hadn't met me, you'd have been poorer by thousands. You want a change."

There was a silence, Her head was drooped, and Michael could not see the girl's face, but when she spoke, there was that note of viciousness in her voice which told him her state of mind.

"You want a change too, perhaps! I could tell things about you that wouldn't look good in print, and you'd have a change too! Get that in your mind, Gregory Penne! I'm not a fool – I've seen things and heard things, and I can put two and two together. You think I want a change, do you – I do! I want friends who aren't murderers – "

He sprang at her, his big hand covering her mouth.

"You little devil!" he hissed, and at that instant somebody must have knocked, for he turned to the door and said something in the native dialect.

The answer was inaudible to Mike.

"Listen." Gregory was speaking to the girl in a calmer tone. "Foss is waiting to see me, and I'll discuss this little matter with you afterwards."

He released her, and, going to his desk, touched the spring that operated the mechanism of the secret door that led to Bhag's quarters.

"Go in there and wait," he said. "I'll not keep you longer than five minutes."

She looked suspiciously at the door which had suddenly opened in the panelling.

"No," she said, "I'll go home. Tomorrow will do. I'm sorry I got rough, Gregory, but you madden me sometimes."

"Go in there !"

He pointed to the den, his face working.

"I'll not!" Her face was white. "You beast, don't you think I know? That is Bhag's den! Oh, you beast!"

His face was horrible to see. It was as though all the foulness in his mind found expression in the demoniacal grimace.

Breathless, terrified, the girl stared at him, shrinking back against the wall. Presently Gregory mastered himself.

"Then go into the little drawing-room," he said huskily.

Mike had time to switch out the lights and flatten himself against the wall, when the door of the room was flung open and the girl thrust in.

"It is dark!" she wailed.

"You'll find the switches!"

The door banged.

Michael Brixan was in a dilemma. He could see her figure groping along the wall, and stealthily he moved to avoid her. In doing so he stumbled over a stool.

"Who's there?" she screamed. "Gregory! Don't let him touch me, Gregory!"

Again the piercing scream.

Mike leapt past her and through the open window, and, the sound of her shrill agony in his ears, fled along the hedge. Swift as he was, something sped more quickly in pursuit, a great, twittering something that ran bent double on hands and feet. The detective heard and guessed. From what secret hiding-place Bhag had appeared, whether he was in the grounds at the moment Mike jumped, he had no time even to guess. He felt a curious lightness of pocket at that moment and thrust in his hand. His pistol was gone. It must have fallen when he jumped.

He could hear the pad of feet behind him as he darted at a tangent across the field, blundering over the cabbage rows, slipping in furrows, the great beast growing closer and closer with every check. Ahead of him the postern. But it was locked, and, even if it had not been, the wall would have proved no obstacle to the ape. The barrier of the wall held Michael. Breathless, turning to face his pursuer, in the darkness he saw the green eyes shining like two evil stars.

A NARROW ESCAPE

Michael Brixan braced himself for the supreme and futile struggle. And then, to his amazement, the ape stopped, and his bird noise became a harsh chatter. Raising himself erect, he beat quickly on his great hairy chest, and the sound of the hollow drumming was awful.

Yet through that sound and above it, Michael heard a curious hiss – it was the faint note of escaping steam, and he looked round. On the top of the wall squatted a man, and Michael knew him at once. It was the brown-faced stranger he had seen that day in Chichester.

The drumming and the hissing grew louder and then Michael saw a bright, curved thing in the brown man's hand. It was a sword, the replica of that which hung above Sir Gregory's fireplace.

He was still wondering when the brown man dropped lightly to the ground, and Bhag, with a squeal that was almost human, turned and fled. Michael watched the Thing, fascinated, until it disappeared into the darkness.

"My friend," said Michael in Dutch, "you came at a good moment."

He turned, but the brown man had vanished as though the earth had swallowed him. Shading his eyes against the starlight, he presently discerned a dark shape moving swiftly in the shadow of the wall. For a second he was inclined to follow and question the brown man, but decided upon another course. With some difficulty he surmounted the wall and dropped to the other side. Then, tidying himself as well as he could, he made the long circuit to the gate of Griff Towers, and boldly walked up to the house, whistling as he went.

There was nobody in sight as he crossed the "parade ground," and his first step was to search for and find his pistol.

He must know that the girl was safe before he left the place. He had seen her car waiting on the road outside. His hand was raised to the bell when he heard footsteps in the hall, and listened intently: there was no doubt that one of the voices was Stella Mendoza's, and he drew back again to cover.

The girl came out, followed by Sir Gregory, and from their tone, a stranger unacquainted with the circumstances of their meeting might have imagined that the visit had been a very ordinary one, in spite of the lateness of the hour.

"Good night, Sir Gregory," said the girl, almost sweetly. "I will see you tomorrow."

"Come to lunch," said Gregory's voice, "and bring your friend. Shall I walk with you to the car?"

"No, thank you," she said hastily.

Michael watched her till she was out of sight, but long before then the big door of Griff Towers had closed, and the familiar rattle of chains told him that it was closed finally.

Where was Foss? He must have gone earlier, if Foss it was. Michael waited till all was quiet, and then, tip-toeing across the gravel, followed the girl. He looked about for the little brown man, but he was not in sight. And then he remembered that he had left the hook ladder hanging to the window on the stairs, and went back to retrieve it. He found the ladder as it had been left, unscrewed and packed it in the canvas bag, and five minutes later he was taking his motor-cycle from its place of concealment.

A yellow light showed in the window of Mr Longvale's dining-room, and Michael had half a mind to call upon him. He could tell him, at any rate, something of that oval-faced girl in the upper room of the tower. Instead, he decided to go home. He was tired with the night's work, a little disappointed. The tower had not revealed as tremendous a secret as he had hoped. The girl was a prisoner, obviously; had been kidnapped for Sir Gregory's pleasure, and brought to England on his yacht. Such things had happened; there had been a case in the courts on curiously parallel lines only a few months before. At any rate, it did not seem worthwhile to put off his bedtime.

He had a hot bath, made himself some chocolate and, before retiring, sat down to sum up his day's experience. And in the light of recent happenings he was less confident that his first solution of the Head-Hunter mystery was the correct one. And the more he thought, the less satisfied he was, till at last, in sheer disgust at his own vacillation of mind, he turned out the light and went to bed.

He was sleeping peacefully and late the next morning when an unexpected visitor arrived, and Michael sat up in bed and rubbed his eyes.

"I've either got nightmare or it's Staines," he said.

Major Staines smiled cheerfully.

"You're awake and normal," he said.

"Has anything happened?" asked Michael, springing out of bed.

"Nothing, only there was a late dance last night and an early train this morning, and I decided to atone for my frivolity by coming down and seeing how far you had got in the Elmer case."

"Elmer case?" Michael frowned. "Good Lord! I'd almost forgotten poor Elmer!"

"Here's something to remind you," said Staines.

He fished from his pocket a newspaper cutting. Michael took it and read:

Is your trouble of mind or body incurable? Do you hesitate on the brink of the abyss? Does courage fail you? Write to Benefactor, Box —

"What is this?" asked Michael, frowning.

"It was found in the pocket of an old waistcoat that Elmer was wearing a few days before he disappeared. Mrs Elmer was going through his clothes with the idea of selling them, when she found this. It appeared in the *Morning Telegram* of the fourteenth – that is to say, three or four days before Elmer vanished. The box number at the end, of course, is the box number of the newspaper to which replies were sent. There is a record that four letters reached the 'Benefactor,' who, so far as we have been able to discover, had these particular letters readdressed to a little shop in Stibbington Street, London. Here they were collected by a woman, evidently of the working class, and probably a charlady from the appearance which has been circulated. Beyond that, no further trace has been obtainable. Similar advertisements have been found by search in other newspapers, but in these cases the letters were sent to an accommodation address in South London, where apparently the same woman collected them. With every new advertisement the advertiser changes his address. She was a stranger to each neighbourhood, by the way; and from what shopkeepers have told Scotland Yard, she seemed to be a little off her head, for she was in the habit of mumbling and talking to herself. Her name is Stivins – at least, that is the name she always gave. And the notes she brought were usually signed 'Mark' – that is to say, the notes authorizing the shopkeepers to hand the letters to her. That she is a native of London there is no doubt, but so far the police have not trailed her."

"And suppose they do?" asked Michael. "Do you connect the advertisement with the murders?"

"We do and we do not," replied the other. "I merely point out that this advertisement is a peculiar one, and in all the circumstances a little suspicious. Now what is the theory you wanted to give me?"

For an hour Michael spoke, interrupted at intervals by questions which Staines put to him.

"It is a queer idea, almost a fantastical one," said Staines gravely, "but if you feel that you've got so much as one thread in your hands, go right ahead. To tell you the truth," in a burst of confidence, "I had a horrible feeling that you had fallen down; and since I do not want our department to be a source of amusement to Scotland Yard, I thought I'd come along and give you the result of my own private investigations. I agree with you," he said later, as they sat at breakfast, "that you want to go very, very carefully. It is a delicate business. You haven't told the Scotland Yard men your suspicions?"

Michael shook his head.

"Then don't," said the other emphatically. "They'd be certain to go along and put the person you suspect under arrest, and probably that would destroy the evidence that would convict. You say you have made a search of the house?"

"Not a search: I've made a rough inspection."

"Are there cellars?"

"I should imagine so," said Michael. "That type of house usually has."

"Outhouses where – ?"

Michael shook his head.

"There are none, so far as I have been able to see."

Michael walked down to the railway station with his chief, who told him he was leaving in a much more cheerful frame of mind than he had been in when he arrived.

"There's one warning I'll give to you, Mike," said Staines as the train was about to pull out of the station, "and it is to watch out for yourself! You're dealing with a ruthless and ingenious man. For heaven's sake do not underrate his intelligence. I don't want to wake up one morning to learn that you have vanished from the ken of man."

THE ERASURE

Mike's way back did not lead through the little street where Adele Leamington lived – at least, not his nearest road. Yet he found himself knocking at the door, and learnt, with a sense of disappointment, that the girl had been out since seven o'clock in the morning. Knebworth was shooting on the South Downs, and the studio, when he arrived, was empty, except for Knebworth's secretary and the new scenario editor, who had arrived late on the previous evening.

"I don't know the location, Mr Brixan," said Dicker, the secretary, "but it's somewhere above Arundel. Miss Mendoza was here this morning, asking the same question. She wanted Miss Leamington to go out to lunch with her."

"Oh, she did, did she?" said Michael softly. "Well, if she comes again, you can tell her from me that Miss Leamington has another engagement."

The other nodded wisely.

"I hope she won't keep you waiting," he said. "You never know, when Jack's on location – "

"I did not say she had an engagement with me," said Michael loudly.

"That reminds me, Mr Brixan," said the secretary suddenly. "Do you remember the fuss you made – I mean, there was – about a sheet of manuscript that by some accident had got into Miss Leamington's script?"

Michael nodded.

"Has the manuscript been found?" he asked.

"No, but the new scenario editor tells me that he was looking through the book where Foss kept a record of all the manuscripts that came in, and he found one entry had been blacked out with Indian ink."

"I'd like to see that book," said the interested Michael, and it was brought to him, a large foolscap ledger, ruled to show the name of the submitted scenario, the author, his address, the date received and the date returned. Mike put it down on the table in Knebworth's private office and went carefully through the list of authors.

"If he sent one he has probably sent more," he said. "There are no other erasures?"

The secretary shook his head.

"That is the only one we've seen," he said. "You'll find lots of names of local people – there isn't a tradesman in the place who hasn't written a scenario or submitted an idea since we've been operating."

Slowly Michael's finger went up the column of names. Page after page was turned back. And then his finger stopped at an entry.

"The Power of Fear: Sir Gregory Penne," he read, and looked round at Dicker.

"Did Sir Gregory submit scenarios, Mr Dicker?"

Dicker nodded.

"Yes, he sent in one or two," he said. "You'll find his name farther back in the book. He used to write scenarios which he thought were suitable for Miss Mendoza. He's not the man you're looking for?"

"No," said Michael quickly. "Have you any of his manuscript?"

"They were all sent back," said Dicker regretfully. "He wrote awful mush! I read one of them. I remember Foss trying to persuade old Jack to produce it. Foss made quite a lot of money on the side, we've discovered. He used to take fees from authors, and Mr Knebworth discovered this morning that he once took two hundred pounds from a lady on the promise that he'd get her into the pictures. He wrote Foss a stinging letter this morning about it."

Presently Michael found Sir Gregory's name again. It was not remarkable that the owner of Griff Towers should have submitted a manuscript. There was hardly a thinking man or woman in the world who did not believe he or she was capable of writing for the films.

He closed the book and handed it back to Dicker.

"It is certainly queer, that erased entry. I'll speak to Foss about it as soon as I can find him," he said.

He went immediately to the little hotel where Foss was staying, but he was out.

"I don't think he came home last night," said the manager. "If he did, he didn't sleep in his bed. He said he was going to London," he added.

Michael went back to the studio, for it had begun to rain, and he knew that that would drive the company from location. His surmise was correct: the big yellow char-à-banc came rumbling into the yard a few minutes after he got there. Adele saw him, and was passing with a nod when he called her to him.

"Thank you, Mr Brixan, but we lunched on location, and I have two big scenes to read for tomorrow."

Her refusal was uncompromising, but Michael was not the type who readily accepted a "No."

"What about tea? You've got to drink tea, my good lady, though you have fifty scenes to study. And you can't read and eat too. If you do, you'll get indigestion, and if you get indigestion – "

She laughed.

"If my landlady will loan me her parlour, you may come to tea at half-past four," she said; "and if you have another engagement at five o'clock, you'll be able to meet it."

Jack Knebworth was waiting for him when he went into the studio.

"Heard about that entry in the scenario book?" he asked. "I see you have. What do you think of it?" Without waiting for a reply: "It looks queer to me. Foss was an unmitigated liar. That fellow couldn't see straight. I've got a little bone to pick with him on the matter of a fee he accepted from a screen-struck lady who wished to be featured in one of my productions."

"How's the girl?" asked Michael.

"You mean Adele? Really, she's wonderful, Brixan! I'm touching wood all the time" – he put his hand on the table piously – "because I know that there's a big shock coming to me somewhere and somehow. Those things do not happen in real life. The only stars that are born in a night are the fireworks produced by crazy vice-presidents who have promised to do something for Mamie and can't break their word. And Mamie, supported by six hundred extras and half a million dollars' worth of sets, two chariot races and the fall of Babylon, all produced regardless of expense, manages to get over by giving a fine imitation of what the Queen of Persia would look like if she'd been born a chorus girl and trained as a mannequin. And she's either got so few clothes that you don't look at her face, or so many clothes that you don't notice her acting.

"Those kind of stars are like the dust of the Milky Way: there is so much splendour all round them that it wouldn't matter if they weren't there at all. But this girl Leamington, she's getting over entirely and absolutely by sheer, unadulterated grey matter. I tell you, Brixan, it's not right. These things do not happen except in the imagination of press agents. There's something wrong with that kid."

"Wrong?" said Michael, startled.

Knebworth nodded.

"Something radically wrong. There's a snag somewhere. She's either going to let me down by vanishing before the picture's through, or else she's going to be arrested for driving a car along Regent Street in a highly intoxicated condition!"

Michael laughed.

"I think she'll do neither," he said.

"Heard about Mendoza's new company?" asked old Jack, filling his pipe.

Michael pulled up a chair and sat down.

"No, I haven't."

"She's starting a new production company. There's never a star I've fired that hasn't! It gets all written out on paper, capital in big type, star in bigger! It's generally due to the friends of the star, who tell her that a hundred thousand a year is a cruel starvation wage for a woman of her genius, and she ought to get it all. Generally there's a sucker in the background who puts up the money. As a rule, he puts up all but enough, and then she selects a story where she is never off the screen, and wears a new dress every fifty feet of fillum. If she can't find that sort of story, why, she gets somebody to write her one. The only time you ever see the other members of the company is in the long shots. Halfway through the picture the money dries up, the company goes bust, and all the poor little star gets out of it is the Rolls-Royce she bought to take her on location, the new bungalow she built to be nearer the lot, and about twenty-five per cent of the capital that she's taken on account of royalties."

"Mendoza will not get a good producer in England?"

"She may," nodded Jack. "There *are* producers in this country, but unfortunately they're not the men on top. They've been brought down by the craze for greatness. A man who produces with a lot of capital behind him can get easy money. He doesn't go after the domestic stories, where he'd be found out first time; he says to the money-bags: 'Let's produce the Fall of Jerusalem. I've got a cute idea for building Ezekiel's temple that's never been taken before. It'll only cost a mere trifle of two hundred thousand dollars, and we'll have five thousand extras in one scene, and we'll rebuild the Colosseum and have a hundred real lions in the arena! Story? What do you want a story for? The public love crowds.' Or maybe he wants to build a new Vesuvius and an eruption at the rate of fifty dollars a foot. There's many a big reputation been built up on sets and extras. Come in, Mr Longvale."

Michael turned. The cheery old man was at the door, hat in hand.

"I am afraid I am rather a nuisance," he said in his beautiful voice. "But I came in to see my lawyer, and I could not deny myself the satisfaction of calling to see how your picture is progressing."

"It is going on well, Mr Longvale, thank you," said Jack. "You know Mr Brixan?"

The old man nodded and smiled.

"Yes, I came in to see my lawyer on what to you will seem to be a curious errand. Many years ago I was a medical student and took my final examination, so that I am, to all intents and purposes, a doctor, though I've not practised to any extent. It is not generally known that I have a medical degree and I was surprised last night to be called out by – er – a neighbour, who wished me to attend a servant of his. Now, I am so hazy on the subject that I wasn't quite sure whether or not I'd broken the law by practising without registration."

"I can relieve your mind there, Mr Longvale," said Michael. "Once you are registered, you are always registered, and you acted quite within your rights."

"So my lawyer informed me," said Longvale gravely.

"Was it a bad case?" asked Michael, who guessed who the patient was.

"No, it was not a bad case. I thought there was blood poisoning, but I think perhaps I may have been mistaken. Medical science has made such great advance since I was a young man that I almost feared to prescribe. Whilst I am only too happy to render any service that humanity demands, I must confess that it was rather a disturbing experience, and I scarcely slept all night. In fact, it was a very disturbing evening and night. Somebody, for some extraordinary reason, put a motor-bicycle in my garden."

Michael smiled to himself.

"I cannot understand why. It had gone this morning. And then I saw our friend Foss, who seemed very much perturbed about something."

"Where did you see him?" asked Michael quickly.

"He was passing my house. I was standing at the gate, smoking my pipe, and bade him good night without knowing who he was. When he turned back, I saw it was Mr Foss. He told me he had been to make a call, and that he had another appointment in an hour."

"What time was this?" asked Michael.

"I think it must have been eleven o'clock." The old man hesitated. "I'm not sure. It was just before I went to bed."

Michael could easily account for Foss's conduct. Sir Gregory had hurried him off and told him to come back after the girl had gone.

"My little place used to be remarkable for its quietness," said Mr Longvale, and shook his head. "Perhaps," turning to Knebworth, "when your picture is finished you will be so good as to allow me to see it?"

"Why, surely, Mr Longvale."

"I don't know why I'm taking this tremendous interest," chuckled the old man. "I must confess that, until a few weeks ago, film-making was a mystery to me. And even today it belongs to the esoteric sciences."

Dicker thrust his head in the door.

"Will you see Miss Mendoza?" he asked.

Jack Knebworth's expression was one of utter weariness.

"No," he said curtly.

"She says – " began Dicker.

Only the presence of the venerable Mr Longvale prevented Jack from expressing his views on Stella Mendoza and all that she could say.

"There's another person I saw last night," nodded Mr Longvale. "I thought at first you must be shooting – is that the expression? – in the neighbourhood, but Mr Foss told me that I was mistaken. She's rather a charming girl, don't you think?"

"Very," said Jack dryly.

"A very sweet disposition," Longvale went on, unconscious of the utter lack of sympathy in the atmosphere. "Nowadays, the confusion and hurry which modernity brings in its trail do not make for sweetness of temper, and one is glad to meet an exception. Not that I am an enemy of modernity. To me, this is the most delightful phase of my long life."

"Sweet disposition!" almost howled Jack Knebworth when the old man had taken a dignified farewell. "Did you get that, Brixan? Say, if that woman's disposition is sweet, the devil's made of chocolate!"

105

THE HEAD

When Mike went out, he found Stella at the gate of the studio, and remembered, seeing her, that she had been invited to lunch at Griff Towers. To his surprise she crossed the road to him.

"I wanted to see you, Mr Brixan," she said. "I sent in word to find if you were there."

"Then your message was wrongly delivered to Mr Knebworth," smiled Mike.

She lifted one of her shoulders in demonstration of her contempt for Jack Knebworth and all his works.

"No, it was you I wanted to see. You're a detective, aren't you?"

"I am," said Michael, wondering what was coming next.

"My car is round the corner: will you come to my house?"

Michael hesitated. He was anxious, more than anxious, to speak to Adele, though he had nothing special to tell her, beyond the thing which he himself did not know and she could never guess.

"With pleasure," he said.

She was a skilful motorist, and apparently so much engrossed in her driving that she did not speak throughout the journey. In the pretty little drawing-room from which he had a view of the lovely South Downs, he waited expectantly.

"Mr Brixan, I am going to tell you something which I think you ought to know."

Her face was pale, her manner curiously nervous.

"I don't know what you will think of me when I have told you, but I've got to risk that. I can't keep silence any longer."

106

A shrill bell sounded in the hall.

"The telephone. Will you excuse me one moment?"

She hurried out, leaving the door slightly ajar. Michael heard her quick, angry reply to somebody at the other end of the wire, and then a long interregnum of silence, when apparently she listened without comment. It was nearly ten minutes before she returned, and her eyes were bright and her cheeks flushed.

"Would you mind if I told you what I was going to tell you a little later?" she asked.

She had been on the telephone to Sir Gregory: of that Michael was sure, though she had not mentioned his name.

"There's no time like the present, Miss Mendoza," he said encouragingly, and she licked her dry lips.

"Yes, I know, but there are reasons why I can't speak now. Would you see me tomorrow?"

"Why, certainly," said Michael, secretly glad of his release.

"Shall I drive you back?"

"No, thank you, I can walk."

"Let me take you to the edge of the town I'm going that way," she begged.

Of course she was going that way, thought Michael. She was going to Griff Towers. He was so satisfied on this matter that he did not even trouble to inquire, and when she dropped him at his hotel, she hardly waited for him to step to the sidewalk before the car leapt forward on its way.

"There's a telegram for you, sir," said the porter. He went into the manager's office and returned with a buff envelope, which Michael tore open.

For a time he could not comprehend the fateful message the telegram conveyed. And then slowly he read it to himself.

A head found on Chobham Common early this morning. Come to Leatherhead Police Station at once.

STAINES.

An hour later a fast car dropped him before the station. Staines was waiting on the step.

"Found at daybreak this morning," he said. "The man is so far unknown."

He led the way to an outhouse. On a table in the centre of the room was a box, and he lifted the lid.

Mike took one glance at the waxen face and turned white.

"Good God!" he breathed.

It was the head of Lawley Foss.

CLUES AT THE TOWER

Michael gazed in fascinated horror at the tragic spectacle. Then reverently he covered the box with a cloth and walked out into the paved courtyard.

"You know him?" asked Staines.

Michael nodded.

"Yes, it is Lawley Foss, lately scenario editor of the Knebworth Picture Corporation. He was seen alive last night at eleven o'clock. I myself heard, if I did not see him, somewhere about that time. He was visiting Griff Towers, Sir Gregory Penne's place in Sussex. Was there the usual note?" he asked.

"There was a note, but it was quite unusual."

He showed the typewritten slip: it was in the station inspector's office. One characteristic line, with its ill-aligned letters.

"This is the head of a traitor." That and no more.

"I've had the Dorking police on the phone. It was a wet night, and although several cars passed none of them could be identified."

"Has the advertisement appeared?" asked Michael.

Staines shook his head.

"No, that was the first thing we thought of. The newspapers have carefully observed, and every newspaper manager in the country has promised to notify us the moment such an advertisement is inserted. But there has been no ad. of any suspicious character."

"I shall have to follow the line of probability here," said Michael. "It is clear that this man was murdered between eleven o'clock and three in the morning – probably nearer eleven than three; for if the murderer is located in Sussex, he would have to bring the head to Chobham, leave it in the dark and return before it was light."

His car took Michael back to Chichester at racing pace. Short of the city he turned off the main road, his objective being Griff Towers. It was late when he arrived, and the Towers presented its usual lifeless appearance. He rang the bell, but there was no immediate reply. He rang again, and then the voice of Sir Gregory hailed him from one of the upper windows.

"Who's there?"

He went out of the porch and looked up. Sir Gregory Penne did not recognize him in the darkness, and called again: "Who's there?" and followed this with a phrase which Michael guessed was Malayan.

"It is I, Michael Brixan. I want to see you, Penne."

"What do you want?"

"Come down and I will tell you."

"I've gone to bed for the night. See me in the morning."

"I'll see you now," said Michael firmly. "I have a warrant to search this house."

He had no such warrant, but only because he had not asked for one.

The man's head was hastily withdrawn, the window slammed down, and such a long interval passed that Michael thought that the baronet intended denying him admission. This view, however, was wrong. At the end of a dreary period of waiting the door was opened, and, in the light of the hall lamp, Sir Gregory Penne presented an extraordinary appearance.

He was fully dressed; around his waist were belted two heavy revolvers, but this fact Michael did not immediately notice. The man's head was swathed in bandages; only one eye was visible; his left arm was stiff with a surgical dressing, and he limped as he walked.

"I've had an accident," he said gruffly.

"It looks a pretty bad one," said Michael, observing him narrowly.

"I don't want to talk here: come into my room," growled the man.

In Sir Gregory's library there were signs of a struggle. A long mirror which hung on one of the walls was shattered to pieces; and, looking up, Michael saw that one of the two swords was missing.

"You've lost something," he said. "Did that occur in course of the 'accident'?"

Sir Gregory nodded.

Something in the hang of the second sword attracted Michael's attention, and, without asking permission, he lifted it down from its hook and drew the blade from the scabbard. It was brown with blood.

"What is the meaning of this?" he asked sternly.

Sir Gregory swallowed something.

"A fellow broke into the house last night," he said slowly, "a Malayan fellow. He had some cock and bull story about my having carried off his wife. He attacked me, and naturally I defended myself."

"And had you carried off his wife?" asked Michael.

The baronet shrugged.

"The idea is absurd. Most of these Borneo folk are mad, and they'll run amok on the slightest provocation. I did my best to pacify him –"

Michael looked at the stained sword.

"So I see," he said dryly. "And did you – pacify him?"

"I defended myself, if that's what you mean. I returned him almost as good as he gave. You don't expect me to sit down and be murdered in my own house, do you? I can use a sword as well as any man."

"And apparently you used it," said Michael. "What happened to Foss?"

Not a muscle of Penne's face moved.

"Whom do you mean?"

"I mean Lawley Foss, who was in your house last night."

"You mean the scenario writer? I haven't seen him for weeks."

"You're a liar," said Michael calmly. "He was in here last night. I can assure you on this point, because I was in the next room."

"Oh, it was you, was it?" said the baronet, and seemed relieved. "Yes, he came to borrow money. I let him have fifty pounds, and he went away, and that's the last I saw of him."

111

Michael looked at the sword again.

"Would you be surprised to learn that Foss's head has been picked up on Chobham Common?" he asked.

The other turned a pair of cold, searching eyes upon his interrogator.

"I should be very much surprised," he said coolly. "If necessary, I have a witness to prove that Foss went, though I don't like bringing in a lady's name. Miss Stella Mendoza was here, having a bit of supper, as you probably know, if it was you in the next room. He left before she did."

"And he returned," said Michael.

"I never saw him again, I tell you," said the baronet violently. "If you can find anybody who saw him come into this house after his first visit you can arrest me. Do you think I killed him?"

Michael did not answer.

"There was a woman upstairs in the tower. What has become of her?"

The other wetted his lips before he replied.

"The only woman in the tower was a sick servant: she has gone."

"I'd like to see for myself," said Michael.

Only for a second did the man cast his eyes in the direction of Bhag's den, and then: "All right," he said. "Follow me."

He went out into the corridor and turned, not toward the hall but in the opposite direction. Ten paces farther down he stopped and opened a door, so cunningly set in the panelling, and so placed between the two shaded lights that illuminated the corridor, that it was difficult to detect its presence. He put in his hand, turned on a light, and Michael saw a long flight of stairs leading back toward the hall.

As he followed the baronet, he realized that the "tower" was something of an illusion. It was only a tower if viewed from the front of the house. Otherwise it was an additional two narrow storeys built on one wing of the building.

They passed through a door, up a circular staircase, and came to the corridor where Michael had seen Bhag squatting on the previous night.

"This is the room," said Penne, opening a door.

THE MARKS OF THE BEAST

"On the contrary, it is not the room," said Michael quietly. "The room is at the end of the passage."

The man hesitated.

"Can't you believe me?" he asked in an almost affable tone of voice. "What a sceptical chap you are! Now come, Brixan! I don't want to be bad friends with you. Let's go down and have a drink and forget our past animosities. I'm feeling rotten – "

"I want to see that room," said Michael.

"I haven't the key."

"Then get it," said Michael sharply.

Eventually the baronet found a pass-key in his pocket, and, with every sign of reluctance, he opened the door.

"She went away in a bit of a hurry," he said. "She was taken so ill that I had to get rid of her."

"If she left here because she was ill she went into an institution of some kind, the name of which you will be able to give me," said Michael, as he turned on the light.

One glance at the room told him that the story of her hasty departure may have been accurate. But that the circumstances were normal, the appearance of the room denied. The bed was in confusion; there was blood on the pillow, and a dark brown stain on the wall. A chair was broken; the carpet had odd and curious stains, one like the print of a bare foot. On a sheet was an indubitable hand-print, but such a hand as no human being had ever possessed.

"The mark of the beast," said Michael, pointing. "That's Bhag!"

Again the baronet licked his lips.

"There was a bit of a fight here," he said. "The man came up and pretended to identify the servant as his wife – "

"What happened to him?"

There was no reply.

"What happened to him?" asked Michael with ominous patience.

"I let him go, and let him take the woman with him. It was easier – "

With a sudden exclamation, Michael stooped and picked up from behind the bed a bright steel object. It was the half of a sword, snapped clean in the middle, and unstained. He looked along the blade, and presently found the slightest indent. Picking up the chair, he examined the leg and found two deeper dents in one of the legs.

"I'll reconstruct the scene. You and your Bhag caught the man after he had got into this room. The chair was broken in the struggle, probably by Bhag, who used the chair. The man escaped from the room, ran downstairs into the library and got the sword from the wall, then came up after you. That's when the real fighting started. I guess some of this blood is yours, Penne."

"Some of it!" snarled the other. "All of it, damn him!"

There was a long silence.

"Did the woman leave this room – alive?"

"I believe so," said the other sullenly.

"Did her husband leave your library – alive?"

"You'd better find that out. So far as I know – I was unconscious for half an hour. Bhag can use a sword – "

Michael did not leave the house till he had searched it from attic to basement. He had every servant assembled and began his interrogation. Each of them except one spoke Dutch, but none spoke the language to such purpose that they made him any wiser than he had been.

Going back to the library, he put on all the lights.

"I'll see Bhag," he said.

"He's out, I tell you. If you don't believe me – " Penne went to the desk and turned the switch. The door opened and nothing came out.

A moment's hesitation and Michael had penetrated into the den, a revolver in one hand, his lamp in another. The two rooms were scrupulously clean, though a strange animal smell pervaded everything. There was a small bed, with sheets and blankets and feather pillow, where the beast slept; a small larder, full of nuts; a running water tap (he found afterwards that, in spite of his cleverness, Bhag was incapable of turning on or off a faucet); a deep, well-worn settee, where the dumb servitor took his rest; and three cricket balls, which were apparently the playthings of this hideous animal.

Bhag's method of entering and leaving the house was now apparent. His exit was a square opening in the wall, with neither window nor curtain, which was situated about seven feet from the ground; and two projecting steel rungs, set at intervals between the window and the floor, made a sort of ladder. Michael found corresponding rungs on the garden side of the wall.

There was no sign of blood, no evidence that Bhag had taken any part in the terrible scene which must have been enacted the night before.

Going back to the library, he made a diligent search, but found nothing until he went into the little drawing-room where he had hidden the night before. Here on the window-sill he found traces enough. The mark of a bare foot, and another which suggested that a heavy body had been dragged through the window.

By this time his chauffeur, who, after dropping him at Griff Towers, went on to Chichester, had returned with the two police officers, and they assisted him in a further search of the grounds. The trail of the fugitive was easy to follow: there were bloodstains across the gravel, broken plants in a circular flower-bed, the soft loam of which had received the impression of those small bare feet. In the vegetable field the trail was lost.

"The question is, who carried whom?" said Inspector Lyle, after Michael, in a few words, had told him all that he had learnt at the Towers. "It looks to me as if these people were killed in the house and their bodies carried away by Bhag. There's no trace of blood in his room, which means no more than that in all probability he hasn't been there since the killing," said Inspector Lyle. "If we find the monkey we'll solve this little mystery. Penne is the Head-Hunter, of course," the Inspector went on. "I had a talk with him the other day, and there's something fanatical about the man."

"I am not so sure," said Michael slowly, "that you're right. Perhaps my ideas are just a little bizarre; but if Sir Gregory Penne is the actual murderer, I shall be a very surprised man. I admit," he confessed, "that the absence of any footprints in Bhag's quarters staggered me, and probably your theory is correct. There is nothing to be done but to keep the house under observation until I communicate with headquarters."

At this moment the second detective, who had been searching the field to its farthermost boundary, came back to say that he had picked up the trail again near the postern gate, which was open. They hurried across the field and found proof of his discovery. There was a trail both inside and outside the gate. Near the postern was a big heap of leaves, which had been left by the gardener to rot, and on this they found the impression of a body, as though whoever was the carrier had put his burden down for a little while to rest. In the field beyond the gate, however, the trail was definitely lost.

THE MAN IN THE CAR

Life is largely made up of little things, but perspective in human affairs is not a gift common to youth. It had required a great effort on the part of Adele Leamington to ask a man to tea, but, once that effort was made, she had looked forward with a curious pleasure to the function.

At the moment Michael was speeding to London, she interviewed Jack Knebworth in his holy of holies.

"Certainly, my dear: you may take the afternoon off. I am not quite sure what the schedule was."

He reached out his hand for the written timetable, but she supplied the information.

"You wanted some studio portraits of me – 'stills,' " she said.

"So I did! Well, that can wait. Are you feeling pretty confident about the picture, eh?"

"I? No, I'm not confident, Mr Knebworth; I'm in a state of nerves about it. You see, it doesn't seem possible that I should make good at the first attempt. One dreams about such things, but in dreams it is easy to jump obstacles and get round dangerous corners and slur over difficulties. Every time you call 'camera!' I am in a state of panic, and I am so self-conscious that I am watching every movement I take, and saying to myself 'You're raising your hands awkwardly; you're turning your head with a jerk.' "

"But that doesn't last?" he said sharply, so sharply that she smiled.

"No: the moment I hear the camera turning, I feel that I *am* the character I'm supposed to be."

He patted her on the shoulder.

"That is how you *should* feel," he said, and went on: "Seen nothing of Mendoza, have you? She isn't annoying you? Or Foss?"

"I've not seen Miss Mendoza for days – but I saw Mr Foss last night."

She did not explain the curious circumstances, and Jack Knebworth was so incurious that he did not ask. So that he learnt nothing of Lawley Foss's mysterious interview with the man in the closed car at the corner of Arundel Road, an incident she had witnessed on the previous night. Nor of the white and womanly hand that had waved him farewell, nor of the great diamond which had sparkled lustrously on the little finger of the unknown motorist.

Going home, Adele stopped at a confectioner's and a florist's, collected the cakes and flowers that were to adorn the table of Mrs Watson's parlour. She wondered more than a little just what attraction she offered to this man of affairs. She had a trick of getting outside and examining herself with an impartial eye, and she knew that, by self-repression and almost self-obliteration, she had succeeded in making of Adele Leamington a very colourless, characterless young lady. That she was pretty she knew, but prettiness in itself attracts only the superficial. Men who are worth knowing require something more than beauty. And Michael was not philandering – he was not that kind. He wanted her for a friend at least: she had no thought that he desired amusement during his enforced stay in a very dull town.

Half-past four came and found the girl waiting. At a quarter to five she was at the door, scanning the street. At five, angry but philosophical, she had her tea and ordered the little maid of all work to clear the table.

Michael had forgotten!

Of course, she made excuses for him, only to demolish them and build again. She was hurt, amused and hurt again. Going upstairs to her room, she lit the gas, took the script from her bag and tried to study the scenes that were to be shot on the following day, but all manner of distractions interposed between her receptive mind and the typewritten paper. Michael bulked largely, and the closed car, and Lawley Foss, and that waving white hand as the car drove off.

Curiously enough, her speculations came back again and again to the car. It was new and its woodwork was highly polished and it moved so noiselessly.

At last she threw the manuscript down and rose, with a doubtful eye on the bed. She was not tired; the hour was nine. Chichester offered few attractions by night. There were two cinemas, and she was not in the mood for cinemas. She put on her hat and went down, calling *en route* at the kitchen door.

"I am going out for a quarter of an hour," she told her landlady, who was in an approving mood.

The house was situate in a street of small villas. It was economically illuminated, and there were dark patches where the light of the street lamps scarcely reached. In one of these a motorcar was standing – she saw the bulk of it before she identified its character. She wondered if the owner knew that its tail light was extinguished. As she came up to the machine she identified the car she had seen on the previous night – Foss had spoken to its occupant.

Glancing to the left, she could see nothing of its interior. The blinds on the road side were drawn, and she thought it was empty, and then…

"Pretty lady – come with me!"

The voice was a whisper: she caught the flash and sparkle of a precious stone, saw the white hand on the edge of the half-closed window, and, in a fit of unreasoning terror, hurried forward.

She heard a whirr of electric starter and the purring of engines. The machine was following her, and she broke into a run. At the corner of the street she saw a man and flew toward him, as she made out the helmet of a policeman.

"What's wrong, miss?"

As he spoke, the car flashed past, spun round the corner and was out of sight instantly.

"A man spoke to me – in that car," she said breathlessly.

The stolid constable gazed vacantly at the place where the car had been.

"He didn't have lights," he said stupidly. "I ought to have taken his number. Did he insult you, miss?"

She shook her head, for she was already ashamed of her fears.

"I'm nervy, officer," she said with a smile. "I don't think I will go any farther."

She turned back and hurried to her lodgings. There were disadvantages in starring — even on Jack Knebworth's modest lot. It was nervous work, she thought.

She went to sleep that night and dreamt that the man in the car was Michael Brixan and he wanted her to come in to tea.

It was past midnight when Michael rang up Jack Knebworth with the news.

"Foss!" he gasped. "Good God! You don't mean that, Brixan? Shall I come round and see you?"

"I'll come to you," said Michael. "There are one or two things I want to know about the man, and it will create less of a fuss than if I have to admit you to the hotel."

Jack Knebworth rented a house on the Arundel Road, and he was waiting at the garden door to admit his visitor when Michael arrived.

Michael told the story of the discovery of the head, and felt that he might so far take the director into his confidence as to retail his visit to Sir Gregory Penne.

"That beats everything," said Jack in a hushed tone. "Poor old Foss! You think that Penne did this? But why? You don't cut up a man because he wants to borrow money."

"My views have been switching round a little," said Michael. "You remember a sheet of manuscript that was found amongst some of your script, and which I told you must have been written by the Head-Hunter?"

Jack nodded.

"I'm perfectly sure," Michael went on, "and particularly after seeing the erasure in the scenario book, that Foss knew who was the author of that manuscript, and I'm equally certain that he resolved upon the desperate expedient of blackmailing the writer. If that is the case, and if Sir Gregory is the man – again I am very uncertain on this point – there is a good reason why he should be put out of the way. There is one person who can help us, and that is – "

"Mendoza," said Jack, and the two men's eyes met.

THE HAND

Jack looked at his watch.

"I guess she'll be in bed by now, but it's worthwhile trying. Would you like to see her?"

Michael hesitated. Stella Mendoza was a friend of Penne's, and he was loath to commit himself irretrievably to the view that Penne was the murderer.

"Yes, I think we'll see her," he said. "After all, Penne knows that he is suspected."

Jack Knebworth was ten minutes on the telephone before he succeeded in getting a reply from Stella's cottage.

"It's Knebworth speaking, Miss Mendoza," he said. "Is it possible to see you tonight. Mr Brixan wants to speak to you."

"At this hour of the night?" she said in sleepy surprise. "I was in bed when the bell rang. Won't it do in the morning?"

"No, he wants to see you particularly tonight. I'll come along with him if you don't mind."

"What is wrong?" she asked quickly. "Is it about Gregory?"

Jack whispered a query to the man who stood at his side, and Michael nodded.

"Yes, it is about Gregory," said Knebworth.

"Will you come along? I'll have time to dress."

Stella was dressed by the time they arrived, and too curious and too alarmed to make the hour of the call a matter of comment.

"What is the trouble?" she asked.

"Mr Foss is dead."

"Dead?" She opened her eyes wide. "Why, I only saw him yesterday. But how?"

"He has been murdered," said Michael quietly. "His head has been found on Chobham Common."

She would have fallen to the floor, had not Michael's arm been there to support her, and it was some time before she recovered sufficiently to answer coherently the questions which were put to her.

"No, I didn't see Mr Foss again after he left the Towers, and then I only saw him for a few seconds."

"Did he suggest he was coming back again?"

She shook her head again.

"Did Sir Gregory tell you he was returning?"

"No." She shook her head again. "He told me he was glad to see the last of him, and that he had borrowed fifty pounds until next week, when he expected to make a lot of money. Gregory is like that – he will tell you things about people, things which they ask him not to make public. He is rather proud of his wealth and what he calls his charity."

"You had a luncheon engagement with him?" said Michael, watching her.

She bit her lip.

"You must have heard me talking when I left him," she said. "No, I had no luncheon engagement. That was camouflage, intended for anybody who was hanging around, and we knew somebody had been in the house that night. Was it you?"

Michael nodded.

"Oh, I'm so relieved!" She heaved a deep sigh. "Those few minutes in that dark room were terrible to me. I thought it was – " She hesitated.

"Bhag?" suggested Michael, and she nodded.

"Yes. You don't suspect Gregory of killing Foss?"

"I suspect everybody in general and nobody in particular," said Michael. "Did you see Bhag?"

She shivered.

"No, not that time. I've seen him, of course. He gives me the creeps! I've never seen anything so human. Sometimes, when Gregory was a little – a little drunk, he used to bring Bhag out and make him do tricks. Do you know that Bhag could do all the Malayan exercises with the sword! Sir Gregory had a specially made wooden sword for him, and the way that that awful thing used to twirl it round his head was terrifying."

Michael stared at her.

"Bhag *could* use the sword, then? Penne told me he did, but I thought he was lying."

"Oh, yes, he could use the sword. Gregory taught him everything."

"What is Penne to you?" Michael asked the question bluntly, and she coloured.

"He has been a friend," she said awkwardly, "a very good friend of mine – financially, I mean. He took a liking to me a long time ago, and we've been – very good friends."

Michael nodded.

"And you are still?"

"No," she answered shortly, "I've finished with Gregory, and am leaving Chichester tomorrow. I've put the house in an agent's hands to rent. Poor Mr Foss!" she said, and there were tears in her eyes. "Poor soul! Gregory wouldn't have done it, Mr Brixan, I'll swear that! There's a whole lot of Gregory that's sheer bluff. He's a coward at heart, and though he has done dreadful things, he has always had an agent to do the dirty work."

"Dreadful things like what?"

She seemed reluctant to explain, but he pressed her.

"Well, he told me that he used to take expeditions in the bush and raid the villages, carrying off girls. There is one tribe that have very beautiful women. Perhaps he was lying about that too, but I have an idea that he spoke the truth. He told me that only a year ago, when he was in Borneo, he 'lifted' a girl from a wild village where it was death for a European to go. He always said 'lifted.'"

"And didn't you mind these confessions?" asked Michael, his steely eye upon her.

She shrugged her shoulders.

"He was that kind of man," was all she said, and it spoke volumes for her understanding of her "very good friend."

Michael walked back to Jack Knebworth's house.

"The story Penne tells seems to fit together with the information Mendoza has given us. There is no doubt that the woman at the top of the tower was the lady he 'lifted,' and less doubt that the little brown man was her husband. If they have escaped from the tower, then there should be no difficulty in finding them. I'll send out a message to all stations within a radius of twenty-five miles, and we ought to get news of them in the morning."

"It's morning now," said Jack, looking toward the greying east. "Will you come in? I'll give you some coffee. This news has upset me. I was going to have a long day's work, but I guess we'll have to put it off for a day or so. The company is bound to be upset by this news. They all knew Foss, although he was not very popular with them. It only wants Adele to be off colour to complete our misery. By the way, Brixan, why don't you make this your headquarters? I'm a bachelor; there's a phone service here, and you'll get a privacy at this house which you don't get at your hotel."

The idea appealed to the detective, and it was at Jack Knebworth's house that he slept that night, after an hour's conversation on the telephone with Scotland Yard.

Early in the morning he was again at the Towers, and now, with the assistance of daylight, he enlarged his search, without adding greatly to his knowledge. The position was a peculiar one, as Scotland Yard had emphasized. Sir Gregory Penne was a member of a good family, a rich man, a justice of the peace; and, whilst his eccentricities were of a lawless character, "you can't hang people for being queer," the Commissioner informed Michael on the telephone.

It was a suspicious fact that Bhag had disappeared as completely as the brown man and his wife.

"He hasn't been back all night: I've seen nothing of him," said Sir Gregory. "And that's not the first time he's gone off on his own. He finds hiding-places that you'd never suspect, and he's probably gone to earth somewhere. He'll turn up."

Michael was passing through Chichester when he saw a figure that made him bring the car to a standstill with such a jerk that it was a wonder the tyres did not burst. In a second he was out of the machine and walking to meet Adele.

"It seems ten thousand years since I saw you," he said with an extravagance which at any other time would have brought a smile to her face.

"I'm afraid I can't stop. I'm on my way to the studio," she said, a little coldly, "and I promised Mr Knebworth that I would be there early. You see, I got off yesterday afternoon by telling Mr Knebworth that I had an engagement."

"And had you?" asked the innocent Michael.

"I asked somebody to take tea with me," and his jaw dropped.

"Moses!" he gasped. "I am the villain!"

She would have gone on, but he stopped her.

"I don't want to shock you or hurt you, Adele," he said gently, "but the explanation for my forgetfulness is that we've had another tragedy."

She stopped and looked at him.

"Another?"

He nodded.

"Mr Foss has been murdered," he said.

She went very white.

"When?" Her voice was calm, almost emotionless.

"Last night."

"It was after nine," she said.

His eyebrows went up in surprise.

"Why do you say that?"

"Because, Mr Brixan" – she spoke slowly – "at nine o'clock I saw the hand of the man who murdered him!"

"Two nights ago," she went on, "I went out to buy some wool I wanted. It was just before the shops closed – a quarter to eight, I think. In the town I saw Mr Foss and spoke to him. He was very nervous and restless, and again made a suggestion to me which he had already made when he called on me. His manner was so strange that I asked him if he was in any trouble. He told me no, but he had had an awful premonition that something dreadful was going to happen, and he asked me if I'd lived in Chichester for any length of time, and if I knew about the caves."

"The caves?" said Michael quickly.

She nodded.

"I was surprised. I'd never heard of the caves. He told me there was a reference to them in some old history of Chichester. He had looked in the guide-books without finding anything about them, but apparently there were caves at some time or other near Chellerton, but there was a heavy subsidence of earth that closed the entrance. He was so rambling and so disjointed that I thought he must have been drinking, and I was glad to get away from him. I went on and did my shopping and met one of the extra girls I knew. She asked me to go home with her. I didn't want to go a bit, but I thought if I refused she would think I was giving myself airs, and so I went. As soon as I could, I came away and went straight home.

"It was then nine o'clock and the streets were empty. They are not very well lit in Chichester, but I was able to recognize Mr Foss. He was standing at the corner of the Arundel Road, and was evidently waiting for somebody. I stopped because I particularly did not wish to meet Mr Foss, but I was on the point of turning round when a car drove into the road and stopped almost opposite him."

"What sort of a car?" asked Michael.

"It was a closed landaulette – I think they call them sedans. As it came round the corner its lights went out, which struck me as being curious. Mr Foss was evidently waiting for this, for he went up and leant on the edge of the window and spoke to somebody inside. I don't know what made me do it, but I had an extraordinary impulse to see who was in the car, and I started walking toward them. I must have been five or six yards away when Mr Foss stepped back and the sedan moved on. The driver put his hand out of the window as if he was waving good-bye. It was still out of the window and the only thing visible – the interior was quite dark – when it came abreast of me."

"Was there anything peculiar about the hand?"

"Nothing, except that it was small and white, and on the little finger was a large diamond ring. The fire in it was extraordinary, and I wondered why a man should wear a ring of that kind. You will think I am silly, but the sight of that hand gave me a terrible feeling of fear – I don't know why, even now. There was something unnatural and abnormal about it. When I looked round again, Mr Foss was walking rapidly in the other direction, and I made no attempt to overtake him."

"You saw no number on the car?"

"None whatever." She shook her head. "I wasn't so curious."

"You didn't even see the silhouette of the man inside?"

"No, I saw nothing. His arm was raised."

"What size was the diamond, do you think?"

She pursed her lips dubiously.

"He passed me in a flash, and I can't give you any very accurate information, Mr Brixan. It may be a mistake on my part, but I thought it was as big as the tip of my finger. Naturally I couldn't see any details, even though I saw the car again last night."

She went on to tell him of what happened on the previous night, and he listened intently.

"The man spoke to you – did you recognize his voice?"

She shook her head.

"No – he spoke in a whisper. I did not see his face, though I have an idea that he was wearing a cap. The policeman said he should have taken the number of the car."

"Oh, the policeman said that, did he?" remarked Michael sardonically. "Well, there's hope for him."

For a minute he was immersed in thought, and then: "I'll take you to the studio if you don't mind," said Michael.

He left her to go to her dressing-room, there to learn that work had been suspended for the day, and went in search of Jack.

"You've seen everybody of consequence in this neighbourhood," he said. "Do you know anybody who drives a sedan and wears a diamond ring on the little finger of the right hand?"

"The only person I know who has that weakness is Mendoza," he said.

Michael whistled.

"I never thought of Mendoza," he said, "and Adele described the hand as 'small and womanly.' "

"Mendoza's hand isn't particularly small, but it would look small on a man," said Jack thoughtfully. "And her car isn't a closed sedan, but that doesn't mean anything. By the way, I've just sent instructions to tell the company I'm working today. If we let these people stand around thinking, they'll get thoroughly upset."

"I thought that too," said Michael with a smile, "but I didn't dare make the suggestion."

An urgent message took him to London that afternoon, where he attended a conference of the Big Five at Scotland Yard. And at the end of the two-hour discussion, the conclusion was reached that Sir Gregory Penne was to remain at large but under observation.

"We verified the story about the lifting of this girl in Borneo," said the quiet-spoken Chief. "And all the facts dovetail. I haven't the slightest doubt in my mind that Penne is the culprit, but we've got to walk very warily. I dare say in your department, Captain Brixan, you can afford to take a few risks, but the police in this country never make an arrest for murder unless they are absolutely certain that a conviction will follow. There may be something in your other theory, and I'd be the last man in the world to turn it down, but you'll have to conduct parallel investigations."

Michael ran down to Sussex in broad daylight. There was a long stretch of road about four miles north of Chichester, and he was pelting along this when he became aware of a figure standing in the middle of the roadway with its arms outstretched, and slowed down. It was Mr Sampson Longvale, he saw to his amazement. Almost before the car had stopped, with an extraordinary display of agility Mr Longvale jumped on the running board.

"I have been watching for you this last two hours, Mr Brixan," he said. "Do you mind if I join you?"

"Come right in," said Michael heartily.

"You are going to Chichester, I know. Would you mind instead coming to the Dower House? I have something important to tell you."

The place at which he had signalled the car to stop was exactly opposite the end of the road that led to the Dower House and Sir Gregory's domain. The old man told him that he had walked back from Chichester, and had been waiting for the passing of the car.

"I learnt for the first time, Mr Brixan, that you are an officer of the law," he said, with a stately inclination of his head. "I need hardly tell you how greatly I respect one whose duty it is to serve the cause of justice."

"Mr Knebworth told you, I presume?" said Michael with a smile.

"He told me," agreed the other gravely. "I went in really to seek you, having an intuition that you had some more important position in life than what I had first imagined. I confess I thought at first that you were one of those idle young men who have nothing to do but to amuse themselves. It was a great gratification to me to learn that I was mistaken. It is all the more gratifying" – (Michael smiled inwardly at the verbosity of age) – "because I need advice on a point of law, which I imagine my lawyer would not offer to me. My position is a very peculiar one, in some ways embarrassing. I am a man who shrinks from the eye of the public and am averse from vulgar intermeddling in other people's affairs."

What had he to tell, Michael wondered – this old man, with his habit of nocturnal strolls, might have been a witness to something that had not yet come out.

They stopped at the Dower House, and the old man got out and opened the gate, not closing it until Michael had passed through. Instead of going direct to his sitting-room, he went upstairs, beckoning Michael to come after, and stopped before the room which had been occupied by Adele on the night of her terrible experience.

"I wish you to see these people," said Mr Longvale earnestly, "and tell me whether I am acting in accordance with the law."

He opened the door, and Mike saw that there were now two beds in the room. On one, heavily bandaged and apparently unconscious, was the brown-faced man; on the other, sleeping, was the woman Michael had seen in the tower! She, too, was badly wounded: her arm was bandaged and strapped into position.

Michael drew a long breath.

"That is a mystery solved, anyway," he said. "Where did you find these people?"

At the sound of his voice the woman opened her eyes and frowned at him fearfully, then looked across to the man.

"You have been wounded?" said Michael in Dutch, but apparently her education had been neglected in respect of European languages, for she made no reply.

She was so uncomfortable at the sight of him that Michael was glad to go out of the room. It was not until they were back in his sanctum that Mr Longvale told his story.

"I saw them last night about half-past eleven," he said. "They were staggering down the road, and I thought at first that they were intoxicated, but fortunately the woman spoke, and as I have never forgotten a voice, even when it spoke in a language that was unfamiliar to me, I realized immediately that it was my patient, and went out to intercept her. I then saw the condition of her companion, and she, recognizing me, began to speak excitedly in a language which I could not understand, though I would have been singularly dense if I had had any doubt as to her meaning. The man was on the point of collapse, but, assisted by the woman, I managed to get him into the house and to the room where he now is. Fortunately, in the expectation of again being called to attend her, I had purchased a small stock of surgical dressing and was able to attend to the man."

"Is he badly hurt?" asked Michael.

"He has lost a considerable quantity of blood," said the other, "and, though there seems to be no arteries severed or bones broken, the wounds have an alarming appearance. Now, it has occurred to me," he went on, in his oddly profound manner, "that this unfortunate native could not have received his injury except as the result of some illegal act, and I thought the best thing to do was to notify the police that they were under my care. I called first upon my excellent friend, Mr John Knebworth, and opened my heart to him. He then told me your position, and I decided to wait your return before I took any further steps."

"You have solved a mystery that has puzzled me, and incidentally, you have confirmed a story which I had received with considerable scepticism," said Mike. "I think you were well advised in informing the police – I will make a report to headquarters, and send an ambulance to take these two people to hospital. Is the man fit to be moved?"

"I think so," nodded the old gentleman. "He is sleeping heavily now, and has the appearance of being in a state of coma, but that is not the case. They are quite welcome to stay here, though I have no convenience, and must do my own nursing, which is rather a bother, for I am not fitted for such a strain. Happily, the woman is able to do a great deal for him."

"Did he have a sword when he arrived?"

Mr Longvale clicked his lips impatiently.

"How stupid of me to forget that! Yes, it is in here."

He went to a drawer in an old-fashioned bureau, pulled it open and took out the identical sword which Michael had seen hanging above the mantelpiece at Griff Towers. It was spotlessly clean, and had been so when Mr Longvale took it from the brown man's hands. And yet he did not expect it to be in any other condition, for to the swordsman of the East his sword is his child, and probably the brown man's first care had been to wipe it clean.

Michael was taking his leave when he suddenly asked: "I wonder if it would give you too much trouble, Mr Longvale, to get me a glass of water? My throat is parched."

With an exclamation of apology, the old man hurried away, leaving Michael in the hall.

Hanging on pegs was the long overcoat of the master of Dower House, and beside it the curly-rimmed beaver and a very prosaic derby hat, which Michael took down the moment the old man's back was turned. It had been no ruse of his, this demand for a drink, for he was parched. Only Michael had the inquisitiveness of his profession.

The old gentleman returned quickly to find Michael examining the hat.

"Where did this come from?" asked the detective.

"That was the hat the native was wearing when he arrived," said Mr Longvale.

"I will take it with me, if you don't mind," said Michael after a long silence.

"With all the pleasure in life. Our friend upstairs will not need a hat for a very long time," he said, with a whimsical little smile.

Michael went back to his car, put the hat carefully beside him, and drove into Chichester; and all the way he was in a state of wonder. For inside the hat were the initials "L F." How came the hat of Lawley Foss on the head of the brown man from Borneo?

THE CAVES

Mr Longvale's two patients were removed to hospital that night, and, with a favourable report on the man's condition from the doctors, Michael felt that one aspect of the mystery was a mystery no longer.

His old schoolmaster received a visit that night.

"More study?" he asked good-humouredly when Michael was announced.

"Curiously enough, you're right, sir," said Michael, "though I doubt very much whether you can assist me. I'm looking for an old history of Chichester."

"I have one published in 1600. You're the second man in the last fortnight who wanted to see it."

"Who was the other?" asked Michael quickly.

"A man named Foss — " began Mr Scott, and Michael nodded as though he had known the identity of the seeker after knowledge. "He wanted to know about caves. I've never heard there were any local caves of any celebrity. Now, if this were Cheddar, I should be able to give you quite a lot of information. I am an authority on the Cheddar caves."

He showed Michael into the library, and taking down an ancient volume, laid it on the library table.

"After Foss had gone I looked up the reference. I find it occurs only on one page – 385. It deals with the disappearance of a troop of horsemen under Sir John Dudley, Earl of Newport, in some local trouble in the days of Stephen. Here is the passage." He pointed.

Michael read, in the old-fashioned type:

The noble Earl, deciding to await hiʃ arrival, carried two *companieʃ* of horʃe by night into the great caveʃ which exiʃted in theʃe timeʃ. By the merciful diʃpenʃation of God, in Whoʃe Handʃ we are, there occurred, at eight o'clock in the forenoon, a great landʃlide which entombed and deʃtroyed all theʃe knightʃ and ʃquireʃ, and ʃir John Dudley, Earl of Newport, ʃo that they were never more ʃeen. And the place of thiʃ happening iʃ nine mileʃ in a line from thiʃ ʃame city, called by the Romanʃ Regnum, or Ciffanceaʃter in the ʃaxon faʃhion.

"Have the caves ever been located?"

Mr Scott shook his head.

"There are local rumours that they were used a century and a half ago by brandy smugglers, but then you find those traditions local to every district."

Michael took a local map of Chichester from his pocket, measured off nine miles, and with a pair of compasses encircled the city. He noted that the line passed either through or near Sir Gregory's estate.

"There are two Griff Towers?" he suddenly said, examining the map.

"Yes, there is another besides Penne's place, which is named after a famous local landmark – the real Griffin Tower (as it was originally called). I have an idea it stands either within or about Penne's property – a very old, circular tower, about twenty feet high, and anything up to two thousand years old. I'm interested in antiquities, and I have made a very careful inspection of the place. The lower part of the wall is undoubtedly Roman work – the Romans had a big encampment here; in fact, Regnum was one of their headquarters. There are all sorts of explanations for the tower. Probably it was a keep or blockhouse. The idea I have is that the original Roman tower was not more than a few feet high and was not designed for defence at all. Successive ages added to its height, without exactly knowing why."

Michael chuckled.

"Now if my theory is correct, I shall hear more about this Roman castle before the night is out," he said.

He gathered his trunks from the hotel and took them off to his new home. He found that the dinner-table was laid for three.

"Expecting company?" asked Michael, watching Jack Knebworth putting the finishing touches on the table – he had a bachelor's finicking sense of neatness, which consists of placing everything at equal distance from everything else.

"Yuh! Friend of yours."

"Of mine?"

Jack nodded.

"I've asked young Leamington to come up. And when I see a man of your age turning pink at the mention of a girl's name, I feel sorry for him. She's coming partly on business, partly for the pleasure of meeting me in a human atmosphere. She didn't do so well today as I wanted, but I guess we were all a little short of our best."

She came soon after, and there was something about her that was very sweet and appealing; something that went straight to Michael's heart and consolidated the position she had taken there.

"I was thinking as I came along," she said, as Jack Knebworth helped her off with her coat, "how very unreal everything is – I never dreamt I should be your guest to dinner, Mr Knebworth."

"And I never dreamt you'd be worthy of such a distinction," growled Jack. "And in five years' time you'll be saying, 'Why on earth did I make such a fuss about being asked to a skimpy meal by that punk director Knebworth?'"

He put his hand on her shoulder and led her into the room, and then for the first time she saw Michael, and that young man had a momentary sense of dismay when he saw her face drop. It was only for a second, and, as if reading his thoughts, she explained her sudden change of mien.

"I thought we were going to talk nothing but pictures and pictures!" she said.

"So you shall," said Michael. "I'm the best listener on earth, and the first person to mention murder will be thrown out of the window."

"Then I'll prepare for the flight!" she said good-humouredly. "For I'm going to talk murder and mystery – later!"

Under the expanding influence of a sympathetic environment the girl took on a new aspect, and all that Michael had suspected in her was amply proven. The shyness, the almost frigid reserve, melted in the company of two men, one of whom she guessed was fond of her, while the other – well, Michael was at least a friend.

"I have been doing detective work this afternoon," she said, after the coffee had been served, "and I've made amazing discoveries," she added solemnly. "It started by my trying to track the motorcar, which I guessed must have come into my street through a lane which runs across the far end. It is the only motorcar track I've found, and I don't think there is any doubt it was my white-handed man who drove it. You see, I noticed the back tyre, which had a sort of diamond-shaped design on it, and it was fairly easy to follow the marks. Halfway up the lane I found a place where there was oil in the middle of the road, and where the car must have stood for some time, and there – I found this!"

She opened her little handbag and took out a small, dark-green bottle. It bore no label and was unstoppered. Michael took it from her hand, examined it curiously and smelt. There was a distinctive odour, pungent and not unpleasing.

"Do you recognize it?" she asked.

He shook his head.

"Let me try." Jack Knebworth took the bottle from Michael's hand and sniffed. "Butyl chloride," he said quickly, and the girl nodded.

"I thought it was that. Father was a pharmaceutical chemist, and once, when I was playing in his dispensary, I found a cupboard open and took down a pretty bottle and opened it. I don't know what would have happened to me, only daddy saw me. I was quite a child at the time, and I've always remembered that scent."

"Butyl chloride?" Michael frowned.

"It's known as the 'death drop' or the 'knock-out drop,'" said Knebworth, "and it's a drug very much in favour with sharks who make a business of robbing sailors. A few drops of that in a glass of wine and you're out!"

Michael took the bottle again. It was a commonplace bottle such as is used for the dispensation of poisons, and in fact the word "Poison" was blown into the glass.

"There is no trace of a label," he said.

"And really there is no connection with the mysterious car," admitted the girl. "My surmise is merely guesswork – putting one sinister thing to another."

"Where was it?"

"In a ditch, which is very deep there and is flooded just now, but the bottle didn't roll down so far as the water. That is discovery number one. Here is number two."

From her bag she took a curious-shaped piece of steel, both ends of which had the marks of a break.

"Do you know what that is?" she asked.

"It beats me," said Jack, and handed the find to Michael.

"*I* know what it is, because I've seen it at the studio," said the girl, "and you know too, don't you, Mr Brixan?"

Mike nodded.

"It's the central link of a handcuff," he said, "the link that has the swivel."

It was covered with spots of rust, which had been cleaned off – by the girl, as she told him.

"Those are my two finds. I am not going to offer you my conclusions, because I have none – "

"They may not have been thrown from the car at all," said Michael, "but, as you say, there is a possibility that the owner of the car chose that peculiarly deserted spot to rid himself of two articles which he could not afford to have on the premises. It would have been safer to throw them into the sea, but this, I suppose, was the easier, and, to him, the safer method. I will keep these."

He wrapped them in paper, put them away in his pocket, and the conversation drifted back to picture-taking, and, as he had anticipated: "We're shooting at Griff Tower tomorrow – the real tower," said Jack

Knebworth. "It is one of the landmarks — what is there amusing in Griff Tower?" he demanded.

"Nothing particularly amusing, except that you have fulfilled a prediction of mine," said Michael. "I knew I should hear of that darned old tower!"

THE TOWER

Michael was a little perturbed in mind. He took a more serious view of the closed car than did the girl, and the invitation to the "pretty lady" to step inside was particularly disturbing. Since the events of the past few days it had been necessary to withdraw the detective who was watching the girl's house, and he decided to re-establish the guard, employing a local officer for the purpose.

After he had driven Adele home, he went to the police station and made his wishes known; but it was too late to see the chief constable, and the subordinate officer in charge did not wish to take the responsibility of detaching an officer for the purpose. It was only when Michael threatened to call the chief on the telephone that he reluctantly drew on his reserves and put a uniformed officer to patrol the street.

Back again at Knebworth's house, Michael examined the two articles which the girl had found. Butyl chloride was a drug and a particularly violent one. What use would the Head-Hunter have for that, he wondered.

As for the handcuff, he examined it again. Terrific force must have been employed to snap the connecting links. This was a mystery to him, and he gave it up with a sense of annoyance at his own incompetence.

Before going to bed he received a phone message from Inspector Lyle, who was watching Griff Towers. There was nothing new to report, and apparently life was pursuing its normal round. The inspector had been invited into the house by Sir Gregory, who had told him that Bhag was still missing.

"I'll keep you there tonight," said Michael. "Tomorrow we will lift the watch. Scotland Yard is satisfied that Sir Gregory had nothing to do with Foss's death."

A grunt from the other end of the phone expressed the inspector's disagreement with that view.

"He's in it somehow," he said. "By the way, I've found a bloodstained derby hat in the field outside the grounds. It has the name of Chi Li Stores, Tjandi, inside."

This was news indeed.

"Let me see it in the morning," said Michael after long cogitation.

Soon after breakfast the next morning the hat came and was inspected. Knebworth, who had heard most of the story from Michael, examined the new clue curiously.

"If the coon wore Lawley's hat when he arrived at Mr Longvale's, where, in the name of fate, did the change take place? It must have been somewhere between the Towers and the old man's house, unless – "

"Unless what?" asked Michael. He had a great respect for Knebworth's shrewd judgment.

"Unless the change took place at Sir Gregory's house. You see that, although it is bloodstained, there are no cuts in it. Which is rum."

"Very rum," agreed Mike ruefully. "And yet, if my first theory was correct, the explanation is simple."

He did not tell his host what his theory was.

Accompanying Knebworth to the studio, he watched the char-à-banc drive off, wishing that he had some excuse and the leisure to accompany them on their expedition. It was a carefree, cheery throng, and its very association was a tonic to his spirits.

He put through his usual call to London. There was no news. There was really no reason why he should not go, he decided recklessly; and as soon as his decision was taken his car was pounding on the trail of the joy wagon.

He saw the tower a quarter of an hour before he came up to it: a squat, ancient building, for all the world like an inordinately high sheepfold. When he came up to them the char-à-banc had been drawn on to the grass, and the company was putting the finishing touches to its make-up. Adele he did not see at once – she was changing in a little canvas tent, whilst Jack Knebworth and the camera man wrangled over light and position.

Michael had too much intelligence to butt in at this moment, and strolled up to the tower, examining the curious courses which generation after generation had added to the original foundations. He knew very little of masonry, but he was able to detect the Roman portion of the wall, and thought he saw the place where Saxon builders had filled in a gap.

One of the hands was fixing a ladder up which Roselle was to pass. The story which was being filmed was that of a girl who, starting life in the chorus, had become the wife of a nobleman with archaic ideas. The poor but honest young man who had loved her in her youth (Michael gathered that a disconsolate Reggie Connolly played this part) was ever at hand to help her; and now, when shut up in a stone room of the keep, it was he who was to rescue her.

The actual castle tower had been shot in Arundel. Old Griff Tower was to serve for a close-up, showing the girl descending from her prison in the arms of her lover, by the aid of a rope of knotted sheets.

"It's going to be deuced awkward getting down," said Reggie lugubriously. "Of course, they've got a rope inside the sheet, so there's no chance of it breaking. But Miss Leamington is really fearfully awfully heavy! You try and lift her yourself, old thing, and see how you like it!"

Nothing would have given Michael greater pleasure than to carry out the instructions literally.

"It's too robust a part for me, it is really," bleated Reggie. "I'm not a cave-man, I'm not indeed! I've told Knebworth that it isn't the job for me. And besides, why do they want a close-up? Why don't they make a dummy that I could carry and sling about? And why doesn't she come down by herself?"

"It's dead easy," said Knebworth, who had walked up and overheard the latter part of the conversation. "Miss Leamington will hold the rope and take the weight off you. All you've got to do is to look brave and pretty."

"That's all very well," grumbled Reggie, but climbing down ropes is not the job I was engaged for. We all have our likes and our dislikes, and that's one of my dislikes."

"Try it," said Jack laconically.

The property man had fixed the rope to an iron staple which he had driven to the inside of the tower, the top of which would not be shown in the picture. The actual descent had been acted by "doubles" in Arundel on a long shot: it was only the close-up that Jack needed. The first rehearsal nearly ended in disaster. With a squeak, Connolly let go his burden, and the girl would have fallen but for her firm grip on the rope.

"Try it again," stormed Jack. "Remember you're playing a man's part. Young Coogan would hold her better than that!"

They tried again, with greater success, and after the third rehearsal, when poor Reggie was in a state of exhaustion –

"Camera!" said Knebworth shortly, and then began the actual taking of the picture.

Whatever his other drawbacks were, and whatever his disadvantages, there was no doubt that Connolly was an artist. Racked with agony at this unusual exertion though he was, he could smile sweetly into the upturned face of the girl, whilst the camera, fixed upon a collapsible platform, clicked encouragingly as it was lowered to keep pace with the escaping lovers. They touched ground, and with one last languishing look at the girl, Connolly posed for the final three seconds.

"That'll do," said Jack.

Reggie sat down heavily.

"My heavens!" he wailed, feeling his arms painfully. "I'll never do that again, I won't really. I've had as much of that stuff as ever I'm going to have, Mr Knebworth. It was terrible! I thought I should die!"

"Well, you didn't," said Jack goodhumouredly. "Now have a rest, you boys and girls, and then we'll shoot the escape."

The camera was moved off twenty or thirty yards, and whilst Reggie Connolly writhed in agony on the ground, the girl walked over to Michael.

"I'm glad that's over," she said thankfully. "Poor Mr Connolly! The awful language he was using inside nearly made me laugh, and that would have meant that we should have had to take it all over again. But it wasn't easy," she added.

Her own arm was bruised, and the rope had rubbed raw a little place on her wrist. Michael had an insane desire to kiss the raw skin, but restrained himself.

"What did you think of me? Did I look anything approaching graceful? I felt like a bundle of straw!"

"You looked – wonderful!" he said fervently, and she shot a quick glance at him and dropped her eyes.

"Perhaps you're prejudiced," she said demurely.

"I have that feeling too," said Michael. "What is inside?" He pointed.

"Inside the tower? Nothing, except a lot of rock and wild bush, and a pathetic dwarf tree. I loved it."

He laughed.

"Just now you said you were glad it was over. I presume you were referring to the play and not to the interior of the tower?"

She nodded, a twinkle in her eye.

"Mr Knebworth says he may have to take a night shot if he's not satisfied with the day picture. Poor Mr Connolly! He'll throw up his part."

At that moment Jack Knebworth's voice was heard.

"Don't take the ladder, Collins," he shouted. "Put it down on the grass behind the tower. I may have to come up here tonight, so you can leave anything that won't be hurt by the weather, and collect it again in the morning."

Adele made a little face.

"I was afraid he would," she said. "Not that I mind very much – it's rather fun. But Mr Connolly's nervousness communicates itself in some way. I wish you were playing that part."

"I wish to heaven I were!" said Michael, with such sincerity in his voice that she coloured.

Jack Knebworth came toward them.

"Did you leave anything up there, Adele?" he asked, pointing to the tower.

"No, Mr Knebworth," she said in surprise.

"Well what's that?"

He pointed to something round that showed above the edge of the tower top.

"Why, it's moving!" he gasped.

As he spoke a head came slowly into view. It was followed by a massive pair of hairy shoulders, and then a leg was thrown over the wall.

It was Bhag!

His tawny hair was white with dust, his face was powdered grotesquely. All these things Michael noticed. Then, as the creature put out his hand to steady himself, Michael saw that each wrist was encircled by the half of a broken pair of handcuffs!

BHAG'S RETURN

The girl screamed and gripped Michael's arm.

"What is that?" she asked. "Is it the Thing that came to my – my room?"

Michael put her aside gently, and ran toward the tower. As he did so, Bhag took a leap and dropped on the ground. For a moment he stood, his knuckles on the ground, his malignant face turned in the direction of the man. And then he sniffed, and, with that queer twittering noise of his, went ambling across the downs and disappeared over a nearby crest.

Michael raced in pursuit. By the time he came into view, the great ape was a quarter of a mile away, running at top speed, and always keeping close to the hedges that divided the fields he had to cross. Pursuit was useless, and the detective went slowly back to the alarmed company.

"It is only an orang-outang belonging to Sir Gregory, and perfectly harmless," he said. "He has been missing from the house for two or three days."

"He must have been hiding in the tower," said Knebworth, and Michael nodded. "Well, I'm darned glad he didn't choose to come out at the moment I was shooting," said the director, mopping his forehead. "You didn't see anything of him, Adele?"

Michael guessed that the girl was pale under her yellow make-up, and the hand she raised to her lips shook a little.

"That explains the mystery of the handcuffs," said Knebworth.

"Did you notice them?" asked Michael quickly. "Yes, that explains the broken link," he said, "but it doesn't exactly explain the butyl chloride."

He held the girl's arm as he spoke, and in the warm, strong pressure she felt something more than his sympathy.

"Were you a little frightened?"

"I was badly frightened," she confessed. "How terrible! Was that Bhag?"

He nodded.

"That was Bhag," he said. "I suppose he's been hiding in the tower ever since his disappearance. You saw nothing when you were on the top of the wall?"

"I'm glad to say I didn't, or I should have dropped. There are a large number of bushes where he might have been hidden."

Michael decided to look for himself. They put up the ladder and he climbed to the broad top of the tower and looked down. At the base of the stonework the ground sloped away in a manner curiously reminiscent of the shell-holes he had seen during the war in France. The actual floor of the tower was not visible under the hawthorn bushes which grew thickly at the centre. He caught a glimpse of the jagged edges of rock, the distorted branches of an old tree, and that was all.

There was ample opportunity for concealment. Possibly Bhag had hidden there most of the time, sleeping off the effects of his labour and his wounds; for Michael had seen something that nobody else had noticed – the gashed skin, and the ear that had been slashed in half.

He came down the ladder again and rejoined Knebworth.

"I think that finishes our work for today," said Jack dubiously. "I smell hysteria, and it will be a long time before I can get the girls to come up for a night picture."

Michael drove the director back in his car, and all the way home he was considering this strange appearance of the ape. Somebody had handcuffed Bhag: he ought to have guessed that when he saw the torn link. No human being could have broken those apart. And Bhag had escaped – from whom? How? And why had he not returned to Griff Towers and to his master?

When he had dropped the director at the studio he went straight on to Gregory's house, and found the baronet playing clock-golf on a strip of lawn that ran by the side of the house. The man was still heavily bandaged, but he was making good recovery.

"Yes, Bhag is back. He returned half an hour ago. Where he has been, heaven knows! I've often wished that chap could talk, but I've never wished it so much as I do at this moment. Somebody had put irons on him: I've just taken them off."

"Can I see them?"

"You knew it, did you?"

"I saw him. He came out of the old tower on the hill." Michael pointed; from where they stood, the tower was in sight.

"Is that so? And what the devil was he doing there?"

Sir Gregory scratched his chin thoughtfully.

"He's been away before, but mostly he goes to a shoot of mine about three miles away, where there's plenty of cover and no intruders. I discovered that when a poacher saw him, and, like a fool, shot at him – that poacher was a lucky man to escape with his life. Have you found the body of Foss?"

The baronet had resumed his playing, and was looking at the ball at his feet.

"No," said Michael quietly.

"Expect to find it?"

"I shouldn't be surprised."

Sir Gregory stood, his hands leaning on his club, looking across the wold.

"What's the law in this country, suppose a man accidentally kills a servant who tried to knife him?"

"He would have to stand his trial," said Michael, "and a verdict of 'justifiable homicide' would be returned and he would be set free."

"But suppose he didn't reveal it? Suppose he – well, did away with the body – buried it – and let the matter slide?"

"Then he would place himself in a remarkably dangerous position," said Michael. "Particularly" – he watched the man closely – "if a woman friend, who is no longer a woman friend, happened to be a witness or had knowledge of the act."

Gregory Penne's one visible eye blinked quickly, and he went that curious purple colour which Michael had seen before when he was agitated.

"Suppose she tried to get money out of him by threatening to tell the police?"

"Then," said the patient Michael, "she would go to prison for blackmail, and possibly as an accessory to or after the fact."

"Would she?" Sir Gregory's voice was eager. "She would be an accessory if she saw – him cut the man down? Mind you, this happened years ago. There's a Statute of Limitations, isn't there?"

"Not for murder," said Michael.

"Murder! Would you call that murder?" asked the other in alarm. "In self-defence? Rot!"

Things were gradually being made light to Michael. Once Stella Mendoza had called the man a murderer, and Michael's nimble mind, which could reconstruct the scene with almost unerring precision, began to grow active. A servant, a coloured man, probably, one of his Malayan slaves, had run amok, and Penne had killed him – possibly in self-defence – and then had grown frightened of the consequences. He remembered Stella's description – "Penne is a bluffer and a coward at heart." That was the story in a nutshell.

"Where did you bury your unfortunate victim?" he asked coolly, and the man started.

"Bury? What do you mean?" he blustered. "I didn't murder or bury anybody. I was merely putting a hypothetical case to you."

"It sounded more real than hypothesis," said Michael, "but I won't press the question."

In truth, crimes of this character bored Michael Brixan; and, but for the unusual and curious circumstances of the Head-Hunter's villainies, he would have dropped the case almost as soon as he came on to it.

There was yet another attraction, which he did not name, even to himself. As for Sir Gregory Penne, the grossness of the man and his hobbies, the sordid vulgarity of his amours, were more than a little sickening. He would gladly have cut Sir Gregory out of life, only – he was not yet sure.

"It is very curious how these questions crop up," Penne was saying, as he came out of his reverie. "A chap like myself, who doesn't have much to occupy his mind, gets on an abstract problem of that kind and never leaves it. So she'd be an accessory after the fact, would she? That would mean penal servitude."

He seemed to derive a great deal of satisfaction from this thought, and was almost amiable by the time Michael parted from him, after an examination of the broken handcuffs. They were British and of an old pattern.

"Is Bhag hurt very much?" asked Michael as he put them down.

"Not very much; he's got a cut or two," said the other calmly. He made no attempt to disguise the happenings of that night. "He came to my assistance, poor brute! This fellow nearly got him. In fact, poor old Bhag was knocked out, but went after them like a brick."

"What hat was that man wearing – the brown man?"

"Keji? I don't know. I suppose he wore a hat, but I didn't notice it. Why?"

"I was merely asking," said Michael carelessly. "Perhaps he lost it in the caves."

He watched the other narrowly as he spoke.

"Caves? I've never heard about those. What are they? Are there any caves near by?" asked Sir Gregory innocently. "You've a wonderful grip of the topography of the county, Brixan. I've been living here off and on for twenty years, and I lose myself every time I go into Chichester!"

THE ADVERTISEMENT

The question of the caves intrigued Michael more than any feature the case had presented. He bethought himself of Mr Longvale, whose knowledge of the country was encyclopaedic. That gentleman was out, but Michael met him, driving his antique car from Chichester. To say that he saw him is to mistake facts. The sound of that old car was audible long before it came into sight around a bend of the road. Michael drew up, Longvale following his example, and parked his car behind that ancient bus.

"Yes, it is rather noisy," admitted the old man, rubbing his bald head with a brilliant bandana handkerchief. "I'm only beginning to realize the fact of late years. Personally, I do not think that a noiseless car could give me as much satisfaction. One feels that something is happening."

"You ought to buy a — " said Michael with a smile, as he mentioned the name of a famous car.

"I thought of doing so," said the other seriously, "but I love old things – that is my eccentricity."

Michael questioned him upon the caves, and, to his surprise, the old man immediately returned an affirmative.

"Yes, I've heard of them frequently. When I was a boy, my father told me that the country round was honeycombed with caves, and that, if anybody was lucky enough to find them, they would discover great stores of brandy. Nobody has found them, as far as I know. There used to be an entrance over there." He pointed in the direction of Griff Tower. "But many years ago – "

He retold the familiar story of the landslide and of the passing out of two companies of gallant knights and squires, which probably the old man had got from the same source of information as Michael had drawn upon.

"The popular legend was that a subterranean river ran into the sea near Selsey Bill – of course, some distance beneath the surface of the water. But, as you know, country people live on such legends. In all probability it is nothing but a legend."

Inspector Lyle was waiting for the detective when he arrived, with news of a startling character.

"The advertisement appeared in this morning's *Daily Star*," he said.

Michael took the slip of paper. It was identically worded with its predecessor.

Is your trouble of mind or body incurable? Do you hesitate on the brink of the abyss? Does courage fail you? Write to Benefactor, Box –

"There will be no reply till tomorrow morning. Letters are to be readdressed to a shop in the Lambeth Road, and the chief wants you to be ready to pick up the trail."

The trail indeed proved to be well laid. At four o'clock on the following afternoon, a lame old woman limped into the newsagent's shop on the Lambeth Road and inquired for a letter addressed to Mr Vole. There were three waiting for her. She paid the fee, put the letters into a rusty old handbag and limped out of the shop, mumbling and talking to herself. Passing down the Lambeth Road, she boarded a tramcar *en route* for Clapham, and near the Common she alighted and, passing out of the region of middle-class houses, came to a jumble of tenements and ancient tumble-down dwellings.

Every corner she turned brought her to a street meaner than the last, and finally to a low, arched alleyway, the paving of which had not been renewed for years. It was a little cul-de-sac, its houses, built in the same pattern, joined wall to wall, and before the last of these she stopped, took out a key from her pocket and opened the door.

She was turning to close it when she was aware that a man stood in the entrance, a tall, good-looking gentleman, who must have been on her heels all the time.

"Good afternoon, mother," he said.

The old woman peered at him suspiciously, grumbling under her breath. Only hospital doctors and workhouse folk, people connected with charity, called women "mother"; and sometimes the police got the habit. Her grimy old face wrinkled hideously at this last unpleasant thought.

"I want to have a little talk with you."

"Come in," she said shrilly.

The boarding of the passage-way was broken in half a dozen places and was indescribably dirty, but it represented the spirit of pure hygiene compared with the stuffy horror which was her sitting-room and kitchen.

"What are you, horspital or p'lice?"

"Police," said Michael. "I want three letters you've collected."

To his surprise, the woman showed relief.

"Oh, is that all?" she said. "Well, that's a job I do for a gentleman. I've done it for years. I've never had any complaint before."

"What is his name?"

"Don't know his name. Just whatever name happens to be on the letters. I send 'em on to him."

From under a heap of rubbish she produced three envelopes, addressed in typewritten characters. The typewriting Michael recognized. They were addressed to a street in Guildford.

Michael took the letters from her handbag. Two of them he read; the third was a dummy which he himself had written. The most direct cross-examination, however, revealed nothing. The woman did the work, receiving a pound for her trouble, in a letter from the unknown, who told her where the letters were to be collected.

"She was a little mad and indescribably beastly," said Michael in disgust when he reported, "and the Guildford inquiries don't help us forward. There's another agent there, who sends the letters back to London, which they never reach. That is the mystery of the proceeding. There simply isn't such an address at London, and I can only suggest that they are intercepted *en route*. The Guildford police have that matter in hand."

Staines was very worried.

"Michael, I oughtn't to have put you on this job," he said. "My first thoughts were best. Scotland Yard is kicking, and say that the meddling of outsiders is responsible for the Head-Hunter not being brought to justice. You know something of inter-departmental jealousy, and you don't need me to tell you that I'm getting more kicks than I'm entitled to."

Michael looked down at his chief reflectively.

"I can get the Head-Hunter, but more than ever I'm convinced that we cannot convict him until we know a little more about – the caves!"

Staines frowned.

"I don't quite get you, Mike. Which caves are these?"

"There are some caves in the neighbourhood of Chichester. Foss knew about them and suspected their association with the Head-Hunter. Give me four days, Major, and I'll have them both. And if I fail" – he paused – "if I fail, the next time you say good morning to me, I shall be looking up to you from the interior of one of the Head-Hunter's boxes!"

JOHN PERCIVAL LIGGITT

It was the second day of Michael's visit to town, and, for a reason which she could not analyse, Adele felt "out" with the world. And yet the work was going splendidly, and Jack Knebworth, usually sparing of his praise, had almost rhapsodized over a little scene which she had acted with Connolly. So generous was he in his praise, and so comprehensive, that even Reggie came in for his share, and was willing and ready to revise his earlier estimate of the leading lady's ability.

"I'll be perfectly frank and honest, Mr Knebworth," he said, in this moment of candour, "Leamington is good. Of course, I'm always on the spot to give her tips, and there's nothing quite so educative — if I may use the term — "

"You may," said Jack Knebworth.

"Thanks," said Connolly. " — as having a finished artiste playing opposite to you. It doesn't do me much good, but it helps her a lot; it inspires courage and all that sort of thing. And though I've had a perfectly awful, dreadful time, I feel that she pays for the coaching."

"Oh, do you?" growled the old man. "And I'd like to say the same about you, Reggie! But unfortunately, all the coaching you've had or ever will get is not going to improve you."

Reggie's superior smile would have irritated one less equable than the director.

"You're perfectly right, Mr Knebworth," he said earnestly. "I can't improve! I've touched the zenith of my power, and I doubt whether you'll ever look upon the like of me again. I'm certainly the best juvenile lead in this, and possibly in any country. I've had three offers to go to Hollywood, and you'll never believe who is the lady who asked me to play against her – "

"I don't believe any of it," said Jack even-temperedly, "but you're right to an extent about Miss Leamington. She's fine. And I agree that it doesn't do you much good playing against her, because she makes you look like a large glass of heavily diluted beer."

Later in the day, Adele herself asked her grey-haired chief whether it was true that Reggie would soon be leaving England for another and a more ambitious sphere.

"I wouldn't think so," said Jack. "There never was an actor that hadn't a better contract up his sleeve and was ready to take it. But when it comes to a show-down, you find that the contracts they're willing to tear up in order to take something better, are locked away in a lawyer's office and can't be got out. In the picture business all over the world, there are actors and actresses who are leaving by the first boat to show Hollywood how it's done. I guess these liners would sail empty if they waited for 'em! That's all bluff, part of the artificial life of make-believe in which actors and actresses have their being."

"Has Mr Brixan come back?"

He shook his head.

"No, I've not heard from him. There was a tough-looking fellow called at the studio half an hour ago to ask whether he'd returned."

"Rather an unpleasant-looking tramp?" she asked. "I spoke to him. He said he had a letter for Mr Brixan which he would not deliver to anybody else."

She looked through the window which commanded a view of the entrance drive to the studio. Standing outside on the edge of the pavement was the wreck of a man. Long, lank black hair, streaked with grey, fell from beneath the soiled and dilapidated golf cap; he was apparently shirtless, for the collar of his indescribable jacket was buttoned up to his throat; and his bare toes showed through one gaping boot.

He might have been a man of sixty, but it was difficult to arrive at his age. It looked as though the grey, stubbled beard had not met a razor since he was in prison last. His eyes were red and inflamed; his nose that crimson which is almost blue. His hands were thrust into the pockets of his trousers, and seemed to be their only visible means of support, until you saw the string that was tied around his lean waist; and as he stood, he shuffled his feet rhythmically, whistling a doleful tune. From time to time he took one of his hands from his pockets and examined the somewhat soiled envelope it held, and then, as if satisfied with the scrutiny, put it back again and continued his jigging vigil.

"Do you think you ought to see that letter?" asked the girl, troubled. "It may be very important."

"I thought that too," said Jack Knebworth, "but when I asked him to let me see the note, he just grinned."

"Do you know who it's from?"

"No more than a crow, my dear," said Knebworth patiently. "And now let's get off the all-absorbing subject of Michael Brixan, and get back to the fair Roselle. That shot I took of the tower can't be bettered, so I'm going to cut out the night picture, and from now on we'll work on the lot."

The production was a heavy one, unusually so for one of Knebworth's; the settings more elaborate, the crowd bigger than ever he had handled since he came to England. It was not an easy day for the girl, and she was utterly fagged when she started homeward that night.

"Ain't seen Mr Brixan, miss?" said a high-pitched voice as she reached the sidewalk.

She turned with a start. She had forgotten the existence of the tramp.

"No, he hasn't been," she said. "You had better see Mr Knebworth again. Mr Brixan lives with him."

"Don't I know it? Ain't I got all the information possible about him? I should say I had!"

"He is in London: I suppose you know that?"

"He ain't in London," said the other disappointedly. "If he was in London, I shouldn't be hanging around here, should I? No, he left London yesterday. I'm going to wait till I see him."

She was amused by his pertinacity, though it was difficult for her to be amused at anything in the state of utter weariness into which she had fallen.

Crossing the market square, she had to jump quickly to avoid being knocked down by a car which she knew was Stella Mendoza's. Stella could be at times a little reckless, and the motto upon the golden mascot on her radiator – "Jump or Die" – held a touch of sincerity.

She was in a desperate hurry now, and cursed fluently as she swung her car to avoid the girl, whom she recognized. Sir Gregory had come to his senses, and she wanted to get at him before he lost them again. She pulled up the car with a jerk at the gates of Griff Towers, flung open the door and jumped out.

"If I don't return in two hours, you can go into Chichester and fetch the police," she said.

GREGORY'S WAY

Stella had left a note to the same effect on her table. If she did not return by a certain hour, the police were to read the letter they would find on her mantelpiece. She had not allowed for the fact that neither note nor letter would be seen until the next morning.

To Stella Mendoza, the interview was one of the most important and vital in her life. She had purposely delayed her departure in the hope that Gregory Penne would take a more generous view of his obligations, though she had very little hope that he would change his mind on the all-important matter of money. And now, by some miracle, he had relented; had spoken to her in an almost friendly tone on the phone; had laughed at her reservations and the precautions which she promised she would take; and in the end she had overcome her natural fears.

He received her, not in his library, but in the big apartment immediately above. It was longer, for it embraced the space occupied on the lower floor by the small drawing-room; but in the matter of furnishing, it differed materially. Stella had only once been in "The Splendid Hall," as he called it. Its vastness and darkness had frightened her, and the display which he had organized for her benefit was one of her unpleasant memories.

The big room was covered with a thick black carpet, and the floor space was unrelieved by any sign of furniture. Divans were set about, the walls covered with eastern hangings; there was a row of scarlet pillars up both sides of the room, and such light as there was came from three heavily-shaded black lanterns, which cast pools of yellow light upon the carpet but did not contribute to the gaiety of the room.

Penne was sitting cross-legged on a silken divan, his eyes watching the gyrations of a native girl as she twirled and twisted to the queer sound of native guitars played by three solemn-faced men in the darkened corner of the room. Gregory wore a suit of flaming red coloured pyjamas, and his glassy gaze and brute mouth told Stella all that she wanted to know about her evil friend.

Sir Gregory Penne was no less and no more than a slave to his appetites. Born a rich man, he had never known denial of his desires. Money had grown to money in a sort of cellular progression, and when the normal pleasures of life grew stale, and he was satiated by the sweets of his possessions, he found his chiefest satisfaction in taking that which was forbidden. The raids which his agents had made from time to time in the jungles of his second home gave him trophies, human and material, that lost their value when they were under his hand.

Stella, who had visions of becoming mistress of Griff Towers, became less attractive as she grew more complaisant. And at last her attraction had vanished, and she was no more to him than the table at which he sat.

A doctor had told him that drink would kill him – he drank the more. Liquor brought him splendid visions, precious stories that wove themselves into dazzling fabrics of dreams. It pleased him to place, in the forefront of his fuddled mind, a slip of a girl who hated him. A gross bully, an equally gross coward, he could not or would not argue a theme to its logical and unpleasant conclusion. At the end there was always his money that could be paid in smaller or larger quantities to settle all grievances against him.

The native who had conducted Stella Mendoza to the apartment had disappeared, and she waited at the end of the divan, looking at the man for a long time before he took any notice of her. Presently he turned his head and favoured her with a stupid, vacant stare.

"Sit down, Stella," he said thickly, "sit down. You couldn't dance like that, eh? None of you Europeans have got the grace, the suppleness. Look at her!"

The dancing girl was twirling at a furious rate, her scanty draperies enveloping her like a cloud. Presently, with a crash of the guitars, she sank, face downward, on the carpet. Gregory said something in Malayan, and the woman showed her white teeth in a smile. Stella had seen her before: there used to be two dancing girls, but one had contracted scarlet fever and had been hurriedly deported. Gregory had a horror of disease.

"Sit down here," he commanded, laying his hand on the divan.

As if by magic, every servant in the room had disappeared, and she suddenly felt cold.

"I've left my chauffeur outside, with instructions to go for the police if I'm not out in half an hour," she said loudly, and he laughed.

"You ought to have brought your nurse, Stella. What's the matter with you nowadays? Can't you talk anything but police? I want to talk to you," he said in a milder tone.

"And I want to talk to you, Gregory. I am leaving Chichester for good, and I don't want to see the place again."

"That means you don't want to see me again, eh? Well, I'm pretty well through with you, and there's going to be no weeping and wailing and gnashing of teeth on my part."

"My new company – " she began, and he stopped her with a gesture.

"If your new company depends upon my putting up the money, you can forget it," he said roughly. "I've seen my lawyer – at least, I've seen somebody who knows – and he tells me that if you're trying to blackmail me about Tjarji, you're liable to get into trouble yourself. I'll put up money for you," he went on. "Not a lot, but enough. I don't suppose you're a beggar, for I've given you sufficient already to start three companies. Stella, I'm crazy about that girl."

She looked at him, her mouth open in surprise.

"What girl?" she asked.

"Adele. Isn't that her name? – Adele Leamington."

"Do you mean the extra girl that took my place?" she gasped.

He nodded, his sleepy eyes fixed on hers.

"That's it. She's my type, more than you ever were, Stella. And that isn't meant in any way disparaging to you."

She was content to listen: his declaration had taken her breath away.

"I'll go a long way to get her," he went on. "I'd marry her, if that meant anything to her – it's about time I married, anyway. Now you're a friend of hers – "

"A friend!" scoffed Stella, finding her voice. "How could I be a friend of hers when she has taken my place? And what if I were? You don't suppose I should bring a girl to this hell upon earth?"

He brought his eyes around to hers – cold, malignant, menacing.

"This hell upon earth has been heaven for you. It has given you wings, anyway! Don't go back to London, Stella, not for a week or two. Get to know this girl. You've got opportunities that nobody else has. Kid her along – you're not going to lose anything by it. Speak about me; tell her what a good fellow I am; and tell her what a chance she has. You needn't mention marriage, but you can if it helps any. Show her some of your jewels – that big pendant I gave you – " He rambled on, and she listened, her bewilderment giving place to an uncontrollable fury.

"You brute!" she said at last. "To dare suggest that I should bring this girl to Griff! I don't like her – naturally. But I'd go down on my knees to her to beg her not to come. You think I'm jealous?" Her lips curled at the sight of the smile on his face. "That's where you're wrong, Gregory. I'm jealous of the position she's taken at the studio, but, so far as you're concerned" – she shrugged her shoulders – "you mean nothing to me. I doubt very much if you've ever meant more than a steady source of income. That's candid, isn't it?"

She got up from the divan and began putting on her gloves.

"As you don't seem to want to help me," she said, "I'll have to find a way of making you keep your promise. And you did promise me a company, Gregory; I suppose you've forgotten that?"

"I was more interested in you then," he said. "Where are you going?"

"I'm going back to my cottage, and tomorrow I'm returning to town," she said.

He looked first at one end of the room and then at the other, and then at her.

"You're not going back to your cottage; you're staying here, my dear," he said.

She laughed.

"You told your chauffeur to go for the police, did you? I'll tell *you* something! Your chauffeur is in my kitchen at this moment, having his supper. If you think that he's likely to leave before you, you don't know me, Stella!"

He gathered up the dressing-gown that was spread on the divan and slipped his arms into the hanging sleeves. A terrible figure he was in the girl's eyes, something unclean, obscene. The scarlet pyjama jacket gave his face a demoniacal value, and she felt herself cringing from him.

He was quick to notice the action, and his eyes glowed with a light of triumph.

"Bhag is downstairs," he said significantly. "He handles people rough. He handled one girl so that I had to call in a doctor. You'll come with me without – assistance?"

She nodded dumbly; her knees gave way under her as she walked. She had bearded the beast in his den once too often.

Halfway along the corridor he unlocked a door of a room and pushed it open.

"Go there and stay there," he said. "I'll talk to you tomorrow, when I'm sober. I'm drunk now. Maybe I'll send you someone to keep you company – I don't know yet." He ruffled his scanty hair in drunken perplexity. "But I've got to be sober before I deal with you."

The door slammed on her and a key turned. She was in complete darkness, in a room she did not know. For one wild, terrified moment she wondered if she was alone.

It was a long time before her palm touched the little button projecting from the wall. She pressed it. A lamp enclosed in a crystal globe set in the ceiling flashed into sparkling light. She was in what had evidently been a small bedroom. The bedstead had been removed, but a mattress and a pillow were folded up in one corner. There was a window, heavily barred, but no other exit. She examined the door: the handle turned in her grasp; there was not even a keyhole in which she could try her own key.

Going to the window. she pulled up the sash, for the room was stuffy and airless. She found herself looking out from the back of the house, across the lawn to a belt of trees which she could just discern. The road ran parallel with the front of the house, and the shrillest scream would not be heard by anybody on the road.

Sitting down in one of the chairs, she considered her position. Having overcome her fear, she had that in her possession which would overcome Gregory if it came to a fight. Pulling up her skirt, she unbuckled the soft leather belt about her waist, and from the Russian leather holster it supported, she took a diminutive Browning – a toy of a weapon but wholly business-like in action. Sliding back the jacket, she threw a cartridge into the chamber and pulled up the safety catch; then she examined the magazine and pressed it back again.

"Now, Gregory," she said aloud, and at that moment her face went round to the window, and she started up with a scream.

Two grimy hands gripped the bars; glaring in at her was the horrible face of a tramp. Her trembling hand shot out for the pistol, but before it could close on the butt, the face had disappeared; and though she went round to the window and looked out, the bars prevented her from getting a clear view of the parapet along which the uncouth figure was creeping.

THE TRAP THAT FAILED

Ten o'clock was striking from Chichester cathedral when the tramp, who half an hour ago had been peering and prying into the secrets of Griff Towers, made his appearance in the market-place. His clothes were even more dusty and soiled, and a policeman who saw him stood squarely in his path.

"On the road?" he asked.

"Yes," whined the man.

"You can get out of Chichester as quick as you like," said the officer. "Are you looking for a bed?"

"Yes, sir."

"Why don't you try the casual ward at the workhouse?"

"They're full up, sir."

"That's a lie," said the officer. "Now understand, if I see you again I'll arrest you!"

Muttering something to himself, the squalid figure moved on toward the Arundel Road, his shoulders hunched, his hands hidden in the depths of his pockets.

Out of sight of the policeman, he turned abruptly to the right and accelerated his pace. He was making for Jack Knebworth's house. The director heard the knock, opened the door and stood aghast at the unexpected character of the caller.

"What do you want, bo'?" he asked.

"Mr Brixan come back?"

"No, he hasn't come back. You'd better give me that letter. I'll get in touch with him by phone."

The tramp grinned and shook his head.

"No, you don't. I want to see Brixan."

"Well, you won't see him here tonight," said Jack. And then, suspiciously: "My idea is that you don't want to see him at all, and that you're hanging around for some other purpose."

The tramp did not reply. He was whistling softly a distorted passage from the "Indian Love Lyrics," and all the time his right foot was beating the time.

"He's in a bad way, is old Brixan," he said, and there was a certain amount of pleasure in his voice that annoyed Knebworth.

"What do you know about him?"

"I know he's in bad with headquarters – that's what I know," said the tramp. "He couldn't find where the letters went to: that's the trouble with him. But *I* know."

"Is that what you want to see him about?"

The man nodded vigorously.

"I know," he said again. "I could tell him something if he was here, but he ain't here."

"If you know he isn't here," asked the exasperated Jack, "why in blazes do you come?"

"Because the police are chivvying me, that's why. A copper down on the market-place is going to pinch me next time he sees me. So I thought I'd come up to fill in the time, that's what!"

Jack stared at him.

"You've got a nerve," he said in awestricken tones. "And now you've filled in your time and I've entertained you, you can get! Do you want anything to eat?"

"Not me," said the tramp. "I live on the fat of the land, I do!"

His shrill Cockney voice was getting on Jack's nerves.

"Well, good night," he said shortly, and closed the door on his unprepossessing visitor.

The tramp waited for quite a long time before he made any move. Then, from the interior of his cap, he took a cigarette and lit it before he shuffled back the way he had come, making a long detour to avoid the centre of the town, where the unfriendly policeman was on duty.

A church clock was striking a quarter past ten when he reached the corner of the Arundel Road, and, throwing away his cigarette, moved into the shadow of the fence and waited.

Five minutes, ten minutes passed, and his keen eyes caught sight of a man walking rapidly the way he had come, and he grinned in the darkness. It was Knebworth. Jack had been perturbed by the visitor, and was on his way to the police station to make inquiries about Michael. This the tramp guessed, though he had little time to consider the director's movements, for a car came noiselessly around the corner and stopped immediately opposite him.

"Is that you, my friend?"

"Yes," said the tramp in a sulky voice.

"Come inside."

The tramp lurched forward, peering into the dark interior of the car. Then, with a turn of his wrist, he jerked open the door, put one foot on the running board, and suddenly flung himself upon the driver.

"*Mr Head-Hunter, I want you!*" he hissed.

The words were hardly out of his mouth before something soft and wet struck him in the face – something that blinded and choked him, so that he let go his grip and fought and clawed like a dying man at the air. A push of the driver's foot, and he was flung, breathless, to the side-walk, and the car sped on.

Jack Knebworth had witnessed the scene as far as it could be witnessed in the half-darkness, and came running across. A policeman appeared from nowhere, and together they lifted the tramp into a sitting position.

"I've seen this fellow before tonight," said the policeman. "I warned him."

And then the prostrate man drew a long, sighing breath, and his hands went up to his eyes.

"This is where I hand in my resignation," he said, and Knebworth's jaw dropped.

It was the voice of Michael Brixan!

THE SEARCH

"Yes, it's me," said Michael bitterly. "All right, officer, you needn't wait. Jack, I'll come up to the house to get this make-up off."

"For the Lord's sake!" breathed Knebworth, staring at the detective. "I've never seen a man made up so well that he deceived me."

"I've deceived everybody, including myself," said Michael savagely. "I thought I'd caught him with a dummy letter, instead of which the devil caught me."

"What was it?"

"Ammonia, I think – a concentrated solution thereof," said Michael.

It was twenty minutes before he emerged from the bathroom, his eyes inflamed but otherwise his old self.

"I wanted to trap him in my own way, but he was too smart for me."

"Do you know who he is?"

Michael nodded.

"Oh, yes, I know," he said. "I've got a special force of men here, waiting to effect the arrest, but I didn't want a fuss, and I certainly did not want bloodshed. And bloodshed there will be, unless I am mistaken."

"I didn't seem to recognize the car, and I know most of the machines in this city," said Jack.

"It is a new one, used only for these midnight adventures of the Head-Hunter. He probably garages it away from his house. You asked me if I'd have something to eat just now, and I lied and told you I was

169

living on the fat of the land. Give me some food, for the love of heaven!"

Jack went into the larder and brought out some cold meat, brewed a pot of coffee, and sat in silence, watching the famished detective dispose of the viands.

"I feel a man now," said Michael as he finished, "for I'd had nothing to eat except a biscuit since eleven this morning. By the way, our friend Stella Mendoza is staying at Griff Towers, and I'm afraid I rather scared her. I happened to be nosing round there an hour ago, to make absolutely sure of my bird, and I looked in upon her – to her alarm!"

There came a sharp rap at the door, and Jack Knebworth looked up.

"Who's that at this time of night?" he asked.

"Probably the policeman," said Michael.

Knebworth opened the door and found a short, stout, middle-aged woman standing on the doorstep with a roll of paper in her hand.

"Is this Mr Knebworth's?" she asked.·

"Yes," said Jack.

"I've brought the play that Miss Leamington left behind. She asked me to bring it to you."

Knebworth took the roll of paper and slipped off the elastic band which encircled it. It was the manuscript of "Roselle."

"Why have you brought this?" he asked.

"She told me to bring it up if I found it."

"Very good," said Jack, mystified. "Thank you very much."

He closed the door on the woman and went back to the dining-room.

"Adele has sent up her script. What's wrong, I wonder?"

"Who brought it?" asked Michael, interested.

"Her landlady, I suppose," said Jack, describing the woman.

"Yes, that's she. Adele is not turning in her part?"

Jack shook his head.

"That wouldn't be likely."

Michael was puzzled.

"What the dickens does it mean? What did the woman say?"

"She said that Miss Leamington wanted her to bring up the manuscript if she found it."

Michael was out of the house in a second, and, racing down the street, overtook the woman.

"Will you come back, please?" he said, and escorted her to the house again. "Just tell Mr Knebworth why Miss Leamington sent this manuscript, and what you mean by having 'forgotten' it."

"Why, when she came up to you – " began the woman.

"Came up to me?" cried Knebworth quickly.

"A gentleman from the studio called for her, and said you wanted to see her," said the landlady. "Miss Leamington was just going to bed, but I took up the message. He said you wanted to see her about the play, and asked her to bring the manuscript. She had mislaid it somewhere and was in a great state about it, so I told her to go on, as you were in a hurry, and I'd bring it up. At least, she asked me to do that."

"What sort of a gentleman was it who called?"

"A rather stout gentleman. He wasn't exactly a gentleman, he was a chauffeur. As a matter of fact, I thought he'd been drinking, though I didn't want to alarm Miss Leamington by telling her so."

"And then what happened?" asked Michael quickly.

"She came down and got in the car. The chauffeur was already in."

"A closed car, I suppose?"

The woman nodded.

"And then they drove off? What time was this?"

"Just after half-past ten. I remember, because I heard the church clock strike just before the car drove up."

Michael was cool now. His voice scarcely rose above a whisper.

"Twenty-five past eleven," he said, looking at his watch. "You've been a long time coming."

"I couldn't find the paper, sir. It was under Miss Leamington's pillow. Isn't she here?"

"No, she's not here," said Michael quietly. "Thank you very much; I won't keep you. Will you wait for me at the police station?"

171

He went upstairs and put on his coat.

"Where do you think she is?" asked Jack.

"She is at Griff Towers," replied the other, "and whether Gregory Penne lives or dies this night depends entirely upon the treatment that Adele has received at his hands."

At the police station he found the landlady, a little frightened, more than a little tearful.

"What was Miss Leamington wearing when she went out?"

"Her blue cloak, sir," whimpered the woman, "that pretty blue cloak she always wore."

Scotland Yard men were at the station, and it was a heavily loaded car that ran out to Chichester – too heavy for Michael, in a fever of impatience, for the weight of its human cargo checked its speed, and every second was precious. At last, after an eternity of time, the big car swung into the drive. Michael did not stop to waken the lodge-keeper, but smashed the frail gates open with the buffers of his machine, mounted the slope, crossing the gravel parade, and halted.

There was no need to ring the bell: the door was wide open, and, at the head of his party, Mike Brixan dashed through the deserted hall, along the corridor into Gregory's library. One light burnt, offering a feeble illumination, but the room was empty. With rapid strides he crossed to the desk and turned the switch. Bhag's den opened, but Bhag too was an absentee.

He pressed the bell by the side of the fireplace, and almost immediately the brown-faced servitor whom he had seen before came trembling into the room.

"Where is your master?" asked Michael in Dutch.

The man shook his head.

"I don't know," he replied, but instinctively he looked up to the ceiling.

"Show me the way."

They went back to the hall, up the broad stairway on to the first floor. Along a corridor, hung with swords, as was its fellow below, he reached another open door – the great dance hall where Gregory Penne had held revel that evening. There was nobody in sight, and

Michael came out into the hall. As he did so, he was aware of a frantic tapping at one of the doors in the corridor. The key was in the lock: he turned it and flung the door wide open, and Stella Mendoza, white as death, staggered out.

"Where is Adele?" she gasped.

"I want to ask you that," said Michael sternly. "Where is she?"

The girl shook her head helplessly, strove to speak, and then collapsed in a swoon.

He did not wait for her to recover, but continued his search. From room to room he went, but there was no sign of Adele or the brutal owner of Griff Towers. He searched the library again, and passed through into the little drawing-room, where a table was laid for two. The cloth was wet with spilt wine; one glass was half empty – but the two for whom the table was laid had vanished. They must have gone out of the front door – whither?

He was standing tense, his mind concentrated upon a problem that was more vital to him than life itself, when he heard a sound that came from the direction of Bhag's den. And then there appeared in the doorway the monstrous ape himself. He was bleeding from a wound in the shoulder; the blood fell drip-drip-drip as he stood, clutching in his two great hands something that seemed like a bundle of rags. As Michael looked, the room rocked before his eyes.

The tattered, stained garment that Bhag held was the cloak that Adele Leamington had worn!

For a second Bhag glared at the man who he knew was his enemy, and then, dropping the cloak, he shrank back toward his quarters, his teeth bared.

Three times Michael's automatic spat, and the great, man-like thing disappeared in a flash – and the door closed with a click.

Knebworth had been a witness of the scene. It was he who ran forward and picked up the cloak that the ape had dropped.

"Yes, that was hers," he said huskily, and a horrible thought chilled him.

Michael had opened the door of the den, and, pistol in hand, dashed through the opening. Knebworth dared not follow. He stood petrified, waiting, and then Michael reappeared.

"There's nothing here," he said.

"Nothing?" asked Jack Knebworth in a whisper. "Thank God!"

"Bhag has gone – I think I may have hit him; there is a trail of blood, but I may not be responsible for that. He had been shot recently," he pointed to stains on the floor. "He wasn't shot when I saw him last."

"Have you seen him before tonight?"

Michael nodded.

"For three nights he has been haunting Longvale's house."

"Longvale's!"

Where was Adele? That was the one dominant question, the one thought uppermost in Michael Brixan's mind. And where was the baronet? What was the meaning of that open door? None of the servants could tell him, and for some reason he saw that they were speaking the truth. Only Penne and the girl – and this great ape – knew, unless –

He hurried back to where he had left a detective trying to revive the unconscious Stella Mendoza.

"She has passed from one fainting fit to another," said the officer. "I can get nothing out of her except that once she said 'Kill him, Adele.' "

"Then she has seen her!" said Michael.

One of the officers he had left outside to watch the building had a report to make. He had seen a dark figure climbing the wall and disappear apparently through the solid brickwork A few minutes later it had come out again.

"That was Bhag," said Michael. "I knew he was not here when we arrived. He must have come in through the opening while we were upstairs."

The car that had carried Adele had been found. It was Stella's, and at first Michael suspected that the girl was a party to the abduction. He learnt afterwards that, whilst the woman's chauffeur had been in the kitchen, virtually a prisoner, Penne himself had driven the car to the girl's house, and it was the sight of the machine, which she knew belonged to Stella, that had lulled any suspicions she may have had.

Michael was in a condition bordering upon frenzy. The Head-Hunter and his capture was insignificant compared with the safety of the girl.

"If I don't find her I shall go mad," he said.

Jack Knebworth had opened his lips to answer when there came a startling interruption. Borne on the still night air came a scream of agony which turned the director's blood to ice.

"Help, help!"

Shrill as was the cry, Michael knew that it was the voice of a man, and knew that that man was Gregory Penne!

WHAT HAPPENED TO ADELE

There were moments when Adele Leamington had doubts as to her fitness for the profession she had entered; and never were those periods of doubt more poignant than when she tried to fix her mind upon the written directions of the scenario. She blamed Michael, and was immediately repentant. She blamed herself more freely; and at last she gave up the struggle, rolled up the manuscript book, and, putting an elastic band about it, thrust it under her pillow and prepared for bed. She had rid herself of skirt and blouse when the summons came.

"From Mr Knebworth?" she said in surprise. "At this time of night?"

"Yes, miss. He's going to make a big alteration tomorrow and he wants to see you at once. He has sent his car. Miss Mendoza is coming into the cast."

"Oh!" she said faintly.

Then she had been a failure, after all, and had lived in a fool's paradise for these past days.

"I'll come at once," she said.

Her fingers trembled as she fastened her dress, and she hated herself for such a display of weakness. Perhaps Stella was not coming into the cast in her old part; perhaps some new character had been written in; perhaps it was not for "Roselle" at all that she had been re-engaged. These and other speculations rioted in her mind; and she was in the passage and the door was opened when she remembered that Jack Knebworth would want the manuscript. She ran upstairs, and, by an aberration of memory, forgot entirely where the script had been left. At last, in despair, she went down to the landlady.

"I have left some manuscripts which are rather important. Would you bring them up to Mr Knebworth's house when you find them? They're in a little brown jacket – " She described the appearance as well as she could.

It was Stella Mendoza's car; she recognized the machine with a pang. So Jack and she were reconciled!

In a minute she was inside the machine, the door closed behind her, and was sitting by the driver, who did not speak.

"Is Mr Brixan with Mr Knebworth?" she asked.

He did not reply. She thought he had not heard her, until he turned with a wide sweep and set the car going in the opposite direction.

"This is not the way to Mr Knebworth's," she said in alarm. "Don't you know the way?"

Still he made no reply. The machine gathered speed, passed down a long, dark street, and turned into a country lane.

"Stop the car at once!" she said, terrified, and put her hand on the handle of the door.

Instantly her arm was gripped.

"My dear, you're going to injure your pretty little body, and probably spoil your beautiful face, if you attempt to get out while the car is in motion," he said.

"Sir Gregory!" she gasped.

"Now don't make a fuss," said Gregory. There was no mistaking the elation in his voice. "You're coming up to have a little bit of supper with me. I've asked you often enough, and now you are going willy-nilly! Stella's there, so there's nothing to be afraid of."

She held down her fears with an effort.

"Sir Gregory, you will take me back at once to my lodgings," she said. "This is disgraceful of you – "

He chuckled loudly.

"Nothing's going to happen to you; nobody's going to hurt you, and you'll be delivered safe and sound; but you're going to have supper with me first, little darling. And if you make a fuss, I'm going to turn the car into the first tree I see and smash us all up!"

He was drunk – drunk not only with wine, but with the lust of power. Gregory had achieved his object, and would stop at nothing now.

Was Stella there? She did not believe him. And yet it might be true. She grasped at the straw which Stella's presence offered.

"Here we are," grunted Gregory, as he stopped the car before the Towers door and slipped out on to the gravel.

Before she realized what he was doing, he had lifted her in his arms, though she struggled desperately.

"If you scream I'll kiss you," growled his voice in her ear, and she lay passive.

The door opened instantly. She looked down at the servant standing stolidly in the hall, as Gregory carried her up the wide stairway, and wondered what help might come from him. Presently Penne set her down on her feet and, opening a door, thrust her in.

"Here's your friend, Stella," he said. "Say the good word for me! Knock some sense into her head if you can. I'll come back in ten minutes, and we'll have the grandest little wedding supper that any bridegroom ever had."

The door was banged and locked upon her before she realized there was another woman in the room. It was Stella. Her heart rose at the sight of the girl's white face.

"Oh, Miss Mendoza," she said breathlessly, "thank God you're here!"

THE ESCAPE

"Don't start thanking God too soon," said Stella with ominous calm. "Oh, you little fool, why did you come here?"

"He brought me. I didn't want to come," said Adele.

She was half hysterical in her fright. She tried hard to imitate the calm of her companion, biting her quivering lips to keep them still, and after a while she was calm enough to tell what had happened. Stella's face clouded.

"Of course, he took my car," she said, speaking to herself, "and he has caught the chauffeur, as he said he would. Oh, my God!"

"What will he do?" asked Adele in a whisper.

Stella's fine eyes turned on the girl.

"What do you think he will do?" she asked significantly. "He's a beast – the kind of beast you seldom meet except in books – and locked rooms. He'll have no more mercy on you than Bhag would have on you."

"If Michael knows, he will kill him."

"Michael? Oh, Brixan, you mean?" said Stella with newly awakened interest. "Is he fond of you? Is that why he hangs around the lot? That never struck me before. But what does he care about Michael or any other man? He can run – his yacht is at Southampton, and he depends a lot upon his wealth to get him out of these kind of scrapes. And he knows that decent women shrink from appearance in a police court. Oh, he's got all sorts of defences. He's a worm, but a scaly worm!"

"What shall I do?"

Stella was walking up and down the narrow apartment, her hands clasped before her, her eyes sunk to the ground.

"I don't think he'll hurt me." And then, inconsequently, she went off at a tangent: "I saw a tramp at that window two hours ago."

"A tramp?" said the bewildered girl.

Stella nodded.

"It scared me terribly, until I remembered his eyes. They were Brixan's eyes, though you'd never guess it, the make-up was so wonderful."

"Michael? Is he here?" asked the girl eagerly.

"He's somewhere around. That is your salvation, and there's another."

She took down from a shelf a small Browning.

"Did you ever fire a pistol?"

The girl nodded.

"I have to, in one scene," she said a little awkwardly.

"Of course! Well, this is loaded. That" – she pointed – "is the safety catch. Push it down with your thumb before you start to use it. You had better kill Penne – better for you, and better for him, I think."

The girl shrank back in horror.

"Oh, no, no!"

"Put it in your pocket – have you a pocket?"

There was one inside the blue cloak the girl was wearing, and into this Stella dropped the pistol.

"You don't know what sort of sacrifice I'm making," she said frankly, "and it isn't as though I'm doing it for somebody I'm fond of, because I'm not particularly fond of you, Adele Leamington. But I wouldn't be fit to live if I let that brute get you without a struggle."

And then impulsively she stooped forward and kissed the girl, and Adele put her arms about her neck and clung to her for a second.

"He's coming," whispered Stella Mendoza, and stepped back with a gesture.

It was Gregory – Gregory in his scarlet pyjama jacket and purple dressing-gown, his face aflame, his eyes fired with excitement.

"Come on, you!" He crooked his finger. "Not you, Mendoza: you stay here, eh? You can see her after, perhaps – after supper."

He leered down at the shrinking girl.

"Nobody's going to hurt you. Leave your cloak here."

"No, I'll wear it," she said.

Her hand went instinctively to the butt of the pistol and closed upon it.

"All right, come as you are. It makes no difference to me."

He held her tightly by the hand and marched by her side, surprised and pleased that she offered so little resistance. Down into the hall they went, and then to the little drawing-room adjoining his study. He flung open the door and showed her the gaily decorated table, pushing her into the room before him.

"Wine and a kiss!" he roared, as he pulled the cork from a champagne bottle and sent the amber fluid splashing upon the spotless tablecloth. "Wine and a kiss!" He splashed the glass out to her so that it spilt and trickled down her cloak.

She shook her head mutely.

"Drink!" he snarled, and she touched the glass with her lips.

Then, before she could realize what had happened, she was in his arms, his great face pressed down to hers. She tried to escape from the encirclement of his embrace, successfully averted her mouth and felt his hot lips pressing against her cheek.

Presently he let her go, and, staggering to the door, kicked it shut. His fingers were closing on the key handle when: "If you turn that key I'll kill you."

He looked up in ludicrous surprise, and, at the sight of the pistol in the girl's hand, his big hands waved before his face in a gesture of fear.

"Put it down, you fool!" he squealed. "Put it down! Don't you know what you're doing? The damned thing may go off by accident."

"It will not go off by accident," she said. "Open that door."

He hesitated for a moment, and then her thumb tightened on the safety-catch, and he must have seen the movement.

181

"Don't shoot, don't shoot!" he screamed, and flung the door wide open. "Wait, you fool! Don't go out. Bhag is there. Bhag will get you. Stay with me. I'll – "

But she was flying down the corridor. She slipped on a loose rug in the hall but recovered herself. Her trembling hands were working at the bolts and chains; the door swung open, and in another instant she was in the open, free.

Sir Gregory followed her. The shock of her escape had sobered him, and all the tragic consequences which might follow came crowding in upon him, until his very soul writhed in fear. Dashing back to his study, he opened his safe, took out a bundle of notes. These he thrust into the pocket of a fur-lined overcoat that was hanging in a cupboard and put it on. He changed his slippers for thick shoes, and then bethought him of Bhag. He opened the den, but Bhag was not there, and he raised his shaking fingers to his lips. If Bhag caught her!

Some glimmering of a lost manhood stirred dully in his mind. He must first be sure of Bhag. He went out into the darkness in search of his strange and horrible servant. Putting both hands to his mouth, he emitted a long and painful howl, the call that Bhag had never yet disobeyed, and then waited. There was no answer. Again he sent forth the melancholy sound, but, if Bhag heard him, for the first time in his life he did not obey.

Gregory Penne stood in a sweat of fear, but, so standing, recovered some of his balance. There was time to change. He went up to his ornate bedroom, flung off his pyjamas, and in a short space of time was down again in the dark grounds, seeking for the ape.

Dressed, he felt more of a man. A long glass of whisky restored some of his confidence. He rang for the servant who was in charge of his car.

"Have the machine by the postern gate," he said. "Get it there at once. See that the gate is open: I may have to leave tonight."

That he would be arrested he did not doubt. Not all his wealth, his position, the pull he had in the county, could save him. This latest deed of his was something more than eccentricity.

Then he remembered that Stella Mendoza was still in the house, and went up to see her. A glance at his face told her that something unusual had happened.

"Where is Adele?" she asked instantly.

"I don't know. She escaped – she had a pistol. Bhag went after her. God knows what will happen if he finds her. He'll tear her limb from limb. What's that?"

It was the faint sound of a pistol shot at a distance, and it came from the back of the house.

"Poachers," said Gregory uneasily. "Listen, I m going."

"Where are you going?" she asked.

"That's no damned business of yours," he snarled. "Here's some money." He thrust some notes into her hand.

"What have you done?" she whispered in horror.

"I've done nothing, I tell you," he stormed. "But they'll take me for it. I'm going to get to the yacht. You'd better clear before they come."

She was collecting her hat and gloves when she heard the door close and the key turn. Mechanically he had locked her in, and mechanically took no heed of her beating hand upon the panel of the door.

Griff Towers stood on high ground and commanded a view of the by-road from Chichester. As he stood in the front of the house, hoping against hope that he would see the ape, he saw instead two lights come rapidly along the road.

"The police!" he croaked, and went blundering across the kitchen garden to the gate.

AT THE TOWER AGAIN

Adele went flying down the drive, intent only upon one object, to escape from this horrible house. The gates were closed, the lodge was in darkness, and she strove desperately to unfasten the iron catch, but it held.

Looking back toward the oblong of light which represented the tower door, she was dimly aware of a figure moving stealthily along the grass that bordered each side of the roadway. For a moment she thought it was Gregory Penne, and then the true explanation of that skulking shape came to her, and she nearly dropped. It was Bhag!

She moved as quietly as she could along the side of the wall, creeping from bush to bush, but he had seen her, and came in pursuit, moving slowly, cautiously, as though he was not quite sure that she was legitimate prey. Perhaps there was another gate, she thought, and continued, glancing over her shoulder from time to time, and gripping the little pistol in her hand with such intensity that it was slippery with perspiration before she had gone a hundred yards.

Now she left the cover of the wall and came across a meadow, and at first she thought that she had slipped her pursuer. But Bhag seldom went into the open, and presently she saw him again. He was parallel with her, walking under the wall, and showing no sign of hurry. Perhaps, she thought, if she continued, he would drop his pursuit and go off. It might be curiosity that kept him on her trail. But this hope was disappointed. She crossed a stile and followed a path until she realized it was bringing her nearer and nearer to the wall where her watcher was keeping pace with her. As soon as she realized this, she turned abruptly from the path, and found herself walking through dew-laden grasses. She was wet to the knees before she had gone far, but she did not even know this – Bhag had left cover and was following her into the open!

She wondered if the grounds were entirely enclosed by a wall, and was relieved when she came to a low fence. Stumbling down a bank on to a road which was evidently the eastern boundary of the property, she ran at full speed, though where the road led she could not guess. Glancing back, she saw, to her horror, that Bhag was following, yet making no attempt to decrease the distance which separated them.

And then, far away, she saw the lights of a cottage. They seemed close at hand, but were in reality more than two miles distant. With a sob of thankfulness she turned from the road and ran up a gentle slope, only to discover, to her dismay, when she reached the crest, that the lights seemed as far away as ever. Looking back, she saw Bhag, his green eyes gleaming in the darkness.

Where was she? Glancing round, she found an answer. Ahead and to the left was the squat outline of old Griff Tower.

And then, for some reason, Bhag dropped his rôle of interested watcher, and, with a doglike growl, leapt at her. She flew upward toward the tower, her breath coming in sobs, her heart thumping so that she felt every moment she would drop from sheer exhaustion. A hand clutched at her cloak and tore it from her. That gave her a moment's respite. She must face her enemy, or she herself must perish.

Spinning round, her shaking pistol raised, she confronted the monster, who was growling and tearing at the clothing in his hand. Again he crouched to spring, and she pressed the trigger. The unexpected loudness of the explosion so startled her that she nearly dropped the pistol. With a howl of anguish he fell, gripping at his wounded shoulder, but rose again immediately. And then he began to move backward, watching her all the time.

What should she do? In her present position he might creep from bush to bush and pounce upon her at any moment. She looked up at the tower. If she could reach the top! And then she remembered the ladder that Jack Knebworth had left behind. But that would have been collected.

She moved stealthily, keeping her eye upon the ape, and though he was motionless, she knew he was watching her. Then, groping in the grass, her fingers touched the light ladder, and she lifted it without difficulty and placed it against the wall. She had heard Jack say that the ape could not have climbed the tower from the outside without assistance, though it had been an easy matter, with the aid of the trees growing against the wall inside, for him to get out.

Bhag was still visible; the dull glow of his eyes was dreadful to see. With a wild run she reached the top of the ladder and began pulling it up after her. Bhag crept nearer and nearer till he came to the foot of the tower, made three ineffectual efforts to scale the wall and failed. She heard his twitter of rage, and guided the ladder to the inside of the tower.

For a long time they sat, looking at one another, the orang-outang and the girl. And then Bhag crept away. She followed him as far as her keen eyes could distinguish his ungainly shape, waiting until she was certain he had gone, and then reached for the ladder. The lower rung must have caught in one of the bushes below. She tugged, tugged again, tugged for the third time, and it came away so smoothly that she lost her balance. For a second she was holding the top of the wall with one hand, the ladder with the other; then, half-sliding, half-tumbling, she came down with a run, and picked herself up breathless. She could have laughed at the mishap but for the eerie loneliness of her new surroundings. She tried to erect the ladder again, but in the dark it was impossible to get a firm foundation.

There must be small stones somewhere about, and she began to look out for them. She reached the bottom of the circular depression, and pushing aside a bush to make further progress feeling all the time with her feet for a suitable prop, suddenly she slipped. She was dropping down a sloping shaft into the depths of the earth!

THE CAVERN OF BONES

Down, down, down she fell, one hand clawing wildly at the soft earth, the other clenching unconsciously at the tiny pistol. She was rolling down a steep slope. Once her feet came violently and painfully into contact with an out-jutting rock, and the shock and the pain of it turned her sick and faint. Whither she was going she dared not think. It seemed an eternity before, at last, she struck a level floor and, rolling over and over, was brought up against a rocky wall with a jolt that shook the breath from her body.

Eternity it seemed, yet it could not have been more than a few seconds. For five minutes she lay, recovering, on the rock floor. She got up with a grimace of pain, felt her hurt ankle, and worked her foot to discover if anything was broken. Looking up, she saw a pale star above, and, guessing that it was the opening through which she had fallen, attempted to climb back; but with every step she took the soft earth gave under her feet and she slipped back again.

She had lost a shoe: that was the first tangible truth that asserted itself. She groped round in the darkness and found it after a while, half embedded in the earth. She shook it empty, dusted her stockinged foot, and put it on. Then she sat down to wonder what she should do next. She guessed that, with the coming of day, she would be able to examine her surroundings, and she must wait, with what philosophy she could summon, for the morning to break.

It was then that she became conscious that she was still gripping the earth-caked Browning, and, with a half-smile, she cleaned it as best she could, pressed down the safety-catch and, putting the weapon inside her blouse, thrust its blunt nose into the waistband of her skirt.

The mystery of Bhag's reappearance was now a mystery no longer. He had been hiding in the cave, though it was her imagination that supplied the queer animal scent which was peculiarly his.

How far did the cave extend? She peered left and right, but could see nothing; then, groping cautiously, feeling every inch of her way, her hand struck a stone pillar, and she withdrew it quickly, for it was wet and clammy.

And then she made a discovery of the greatest importance to her. She was feeling along the wall when her hand went into a niche, and by the surface of its shelf she knew it was man-fashioned. She put her hand farther along, and her heart leapt as she touched something which had a familiar and homely feel. It was a lantern. Her other hand went up, and presently she opened its glass door and felt a length of candle, and, at the bottom of the lantern, a small box of matches.

It was no miracle, as she was to learn; but for the moment it seemed that that possibility of light had come in answer to her unspoken prayers. Striking a match with a hand that shook so that the light went out immediately, she at last succeeded in kindling the wick. The candle was new, and at first its light was feeble; but presently the wax began to burn, and, closing the lantern door, her surroundings came into view.

She was in a narrow cave, from the roof of which hung innumerable stalactites; but the dripping water which is inseparable from this queer formation was absent at the foot of the opening where she had tumbled. Farther along the floor was wet, and a tiny stream of water ran in a sort of naturally carved tunnel on one side of the path. Here, where the cave broadened, the stalactites were many, and left and right, at such regular intervals and of such even shape that they seemed almost to have been sculptured by human agency, were little caves within caves, narrow openings that revealed, in the light of her lantern, the splendour of nature's treasures. Fairylike grottos, rich with delicate stone traceries; tiny lakes that sparkled in the light of the lantern. Broader and broader grew the cave, until she stood in a huge chamber that appeared to be festooned with frozen lace. And here the floor was littered with queer white sticks. There were thousands of them, of every conceivable shape and size. They showed whitely in the gleam of her lantern, in the crevices of the rocks. She stooped and picked one up, dropping it quickly with a cry of horror. They were human bones!

With a shuddering gasp she half walked, half ran across the great cavern, which began to narrow again and assumed the appearance of that portion of the cave into which she had fallen. And here she saw, in another niche, a second lantern, with new candle and matches. Who had placed them there? The first lantern she had not dared to think about: it belonged to the miraculous category. But the second brought her up with a jerk. Who had placed these lanterns at intervals along the wall of the cave, as if in preparation for an expected emergency? There must be somebody who lived down here. She breathed a little more quickly at the thought.

Going on slowly, she examined every foot of the way, the second lantern, unlighted, slung on her arm. At one part, the floor was flooded with running water; at another, she had to wade through a little subterranean ford, where the water came over her ankle. And now the cave was curving imperceptibly to the right. From time to time she stopped and listened, hoping to hear the sound of a human voice, and yet fearing. The roof of the cave came lower. There were signs in the roof that the stalactites had been knocked off to afford headroom for the mysterious person who haunted these underground chambers.

Once she stopped, her heart thumping painfully at the sound of footsteps. They passed over her head, and then came a curious humming sound that grew in intensity, passed and faded. A motor-car! She was under the road! Of course, old Griff Tower stood upon the hillside. She was now near the road level, and possibly eight or nine feet above her the stars were shining. She looked wistfully at the ragged surface of the roof, and, steeling herself against the terrors that rose within her, she went on. She had need of nerve, need of courage beyond the ordinary.

The cave passage turned abruptly; the little grotto openings in the wall occurred again. Suddenly she stopped dead. The light of the lantern showed into one of the grottos. Two men lay side by side –

She stifled the scream that rose to her lips, pressing her hands tight upon her mouth, her eyes shut tightly to hide the sight. They were dead – headless! Lying in a shallow pool, the petrifying water came dripping down upon them, as it would drip down for everlasting until these pitiful things were stone.

For a long time she dared not move, dared not open her eyes, but at last her will conquered, and she looked with outward calm upon a sight that froze her very marrow. The next grotto was similarly tenanted, only this time there was one man. And then, when she was on the point of sinking under the shock, a tiny point of light appeared in the gloom ahead. It moved and swayed, and there came to her the sound of a fearful laugh.

She acted instantly. Pulling open the door of the lantern, she stooped and blew it out, and stood, leaning against the wall of the cave, oblivious to the grisly relics that surrounded her, conscious only of the danger which lay ahead. Then a brighter light blazed up and another, till the distant spaces wherein they burnt were as bright as day. As she stood, wondering, there came to her a squeal of mortal agony and a whining voice that cried: "Help! Oh, God, help! Brixan, I am not fit to die!"

It was the voice of Sir Gregory Penne.

MICHAEL KNOWS FOR SURE

It was that same voice that had brought Michael Brixan racing across the garden to the postern gate. A car stood outside, its lights dimmed. Standing by its bonnet was a frightened little brown man who had brought the machine to the place.

"Where is your master?" asked Michael quickly.

The man pointed.

"He went that way," he quavered. "There was a devil in the big machine – it would not move when he stamped on the little pedal."

Michael guessed what had happened. At the last moment, by one of those queer mischances which haunt the just and the unjust, the engine had failed him and he had fled on foot.

"Which way did he go?"

Again the man pointed.

"He ran," he said simply.

Michael turned to the detective who was with him.

"Stay here: he may return. Arrest him immediately and put the irons on him. He's probably armed, and he may be suicidal; we can't afford to take any risks."

He had been so often across what he had named the "Back Field" that he could find his way blindfolded, and he ran at top speed till he came to the stile and to the road. Sir Gregory was nowhere in sight. Fifty yards along the road, the lights gleamed cheerily from an upper window in Mr Longvale's house, and Michael bent his footsteps in that direction.

Still no sight of the man, and he turned through the gate and knocked at the door, which was almost immediately opened by the old gentleman himself. He wore a silken gown, tied with a sash about the middle, a picture of comfort, Michael thought.

"Who's that?" asked Mr Sampson Longvale, peering out into the darkness. "Why, bless my life, it's Mr Brixan, the officer of the law! Come in, come in, sir."

He opened the door wide and Michael passed into the sitting-room, with its inevitable two candles, augmented now by a small silver reading-lamp that burnt some sort of petrol vapour.

"No trouble at the Towers, I trust?" said Mr Longvale anxiously.

"There was a little trouble," said Michael carefully. "Have you by any chance seen Sir Gregory Penne?"

The old man shook his head.

"I found the night rather too chilly for my usual garden ramble," he said, "so I've seen none of the exciting events which seem inevitably to accompany the hours of darkness in these times. Has anything happened to him?"

"I hope not," said Michael quietly. "I hope, for everybody's sake, that – nothing has happened to him."

He walked across and leant his elbows on the mantelpiece, looking up at the painting above his head.

"Do you admire my relative?" beamed Mr Longvale.

"I don't know that I admire him. He was certainly a wonderfully handsome old gentleman."

Mr Longvale inclined his head.

"You have read his memoirs?"

Michael nodded, and the old man did not seem in any way surprised.

"Yes, I have read what purport to be his memoirs," said Michael quietly, "but latter-day opinion is that they are not authentic."

Mr Longvale shrugged his shoulders.

"Personally, I believe every word of them," he said. "My uncle was a man of considerable education."

It would have amazed Jack Knebworth to know that the man who had rushed hotfoot from the tower in search of a possible murderer, was at that moment calmly discussing biography; yet such was the incongruous, unbelievable fact.

"I sometimes feel that you think too much about your uncle, Mr Longvale," said Michael gently.

The old gentleman frowned.

"You mean – ?"

"I mean that such a subject may become an obsession and a very unhealthy obsession, and such hero-worship may lead a man to do things which no sane man would do."

Longvale looked at him in genuine astonishment.

"Can one do better than imitate the deeds of the great?" he asked.

"Not if your sense of values hasn't got all tangled up, and you ascribe to him virtues which are not virtues – unless duty is a virtue – and confuse that which is great with that which is terrible."

Michael turned and, resting his palms on the table, looked across to the old man who confronted him.

"I want you to come with me into Chichester this evening."

"Why?" The question was asked bluntly.

"Because I think you're a sick man, that you ought to have care."

The old man laughed and drew himself even more erect.

"Sick? I was never better in my life, my dear sir, never fitter, never stronger!"

And he looked all that he said. His height, the breadth of his shoulders, the healthy glow of his cheeks, all spoke of physical fitness.

A long pause, and then: "Where is Gregory Penne?" asked Michael, emphasizing every word.

"I haven't the slightest idea."

The old man's eyes met his without wavering.

"We were talking about my great-uncle. You know him, of course?" he asked.

"I knew him the first time I saw his picture, and I thought I had betrayed my knowledge, but apparently I did not. Your great-uncle" – Michael spoke deliberately – "was Sanson, otherwise Longval, hereditary executioner of France!"

Such a silence followed that the ticking of a distant clock sounded distinctly.

"Your uncle has many achievements to his credit. He hanged three men on a gallows sixty feet high, unless my memory is at fault. His hand struck off the head of Louis of France and his consort Marie Antoinette."

The look of pride in the old man's face was startling. His eyes kindled, he seemed to grow in height.

"By what fantastic freak of fate you come to have settled in England, what queer kink of mind decided you secretly to carry on the profession of Sanson and seek far and wide for poor, helpless wretches to destroy, I do not know."

Michael did not raise his voice, he spoke in a calm, conversational tone; and in the same way did Longvale reply.

"Is it not better," he said gently, "that a man should pass out of life through no act of his own, than that he should commit the unpardonable crime of self-murder? Have I not been a benefactor to men who dared not take their own lives?"

"To Lawley Foss?" suggested Michael, his grave eyes fixed on the other.

"He was a traitor, a vulgar blackmailer, a man who sought to use the knowledge which had accidentally come to him, to extract money from me."

"Where is Gregory Penne?"

A slow smile dawned on the man's face.

"You will not believe me? That is ungentle, sir! I have not seen Sir Gregory."

Michael pointed to the hearth, where a cigarette was still smouldering.

"There is that," he said. "There are his muddy footprints on the carpet of this room. There is the cry I heard. Where is he?"

Within reach of his hand was his heavy-calibred Browning. A move on the old man's part, and he would lie maimed on the ground. Michael was dealing with a homicidal lunatic of the most dangerous type, and would not hesitate to shoot.

But the old man showed no sign of antagonism. His voice was gentleness itself. He seemed to feel and express a pride in crimes which, to his brain, were not crimes at all.

"If you really wish me to go into Chichester with you tonight, of course I will go," he said. "You may be right in your own estimation, even in the estimation of your superiors, but, in ending my work, you are rendering a cruel disservice to miserable humanity, to serve which I have spent thousands of pounds. But I bear no malice."

He took a bottle from the long oaken buffet against the wall, selected two glasses with scrupulous care, and filled them from the bottle.

"We will drink our mutual good health," he said with his old courtesy, and, lifting his glass to his lips, drank it with that show of enjoyment with which the old-time lovers of wine marked their approval of rare vintages.

"You're not drinking?" he said in surprise.

"Somebody else has drunk."

There was a glass half empty on the buffet: Michael saw it for the first time.

"He did not seem to enjoy the wine."

Mr Longvale sighed.

"Very few people understand wine," he said, dusting a speck from his coat. Then, drawing a silk handkerchief from his pocket, he stooped and dusted his boots daintily.

Michael was standing on a strip of hearthrug in front of the fireplace, his hand on his gun, tense but prepared for the moment of trial. Whence the danger would come, what form it would take, he could not guess. But danger was there – danger terrible and ruthless, emphasized rather than relieved by the suavity of the old man's tone – he felt in the creep of his flesh.

"You see, my dear sir," Longvale went on, still dusting his boots.

And then, before Michael could realize what had happened, he had grasped the end of the rug on which the detective was standing and pulled it with a quick jerk toward him. Before he could balance himself, Michael had fallen with a crash to the floor, his head striking the oaken panelling, his pistol sliding along the polished floor. In a flash, the old man was on him, had flung him over on his face and dragged his hands behind him. Michael tried to struggle, but he was as a child in that powerful grip, placed at such a disadvantage as he was. He felt the touch of cold steel on his wrists, there was a click, and, exerting all his strength, he tried to pull his other hand away. But gradually, slowly, it was forced back, and the second cuff snapped.

There were footsteps on the path outside the cottage. The old man straightened himself to pull off his silken gown and wrapped it round and round the detective's head, and then a knock came at the door. One glance to see that his prisoner was safe, and Longvale extinguished the lamp, blew out one of the candles, and carried the other into the passage. He was in his shirt-sleeves, and the Scotland Yard officer, who was the caller, apologized for disturbing a man who had apparently been brought down from his bedroom to answer the knock.

"Have you seen Mr Brixan?"

"Mr Brixan? Yes, he was here a few minutes ago. He went on to Chichester."

Michael heard the voices, but could not distinguish what was being said. The silken wrapper about his head was suffocating him, and he was losing his senses when the old man came back alone, unfastened the gown, and put it on himself.

"If you make a noise I will sew your lips together," he said, so naturally and good-naturedly that it seemed impossible he would carry his threat into execution. But Michael knew that he was giving chapter and verse; he was threatening that which his ancestor had often performed. That beautiful old man, nicknamed by the gallants of Louis' court "Monsieur de Paris," had broken and hanged and beheaded, but he had also tortured men. There were smoke-blackened rooms in the old Bastille where that venerable old hangman had performed nameless duties without blenching.

"I am sorry in many ways that you must go on," said the old man, with genuine regret in his voice. "You are a young man for whom I have a great deal of respect. The law to me is sacred, and its officers have an especially privileged place in my affections."

He pulled open a drawer of the buffet and took out a large serviette, folded it with great care and fixed it tightly about Michael's mouth. Then he raised him up and sat him on a chair.

"If I were a young and agile man, I would have a jest which would have pleased my uncle Charles Henry. I would fix your head on the top of the gates of Scotland Yard! I've often examined the gates with that idea in my mind. Not that I thought of you, but that some day providence might send me a very high official, a Minister, even a Prime Minister. My uncle, as you know, was privileged to destroy kings and leaders of parties – Danton, Robespierre, every great leader save Murat. Danton was the greatest of them all."

There was an excellent reason why Michael should not answer. But he was his own cool self again, and though his head was aching from the violent knock it had received, his mind was clear. He was waiting now for the next move, and suspected he would not be kept waiting long. What scenes had this long dining-room witnessed! What moments of agony, mental and physical! It was the very antechamber to death.

Here, then, Bhag must have been rendered momentarily unconscious. Michael guessed the lure of drugged wine, that butyl chloride which was part of the murderer's equipment. But for once Longvale had misjudged the strength of his prey. Bhag must have followed the brown folk to Dower House – the man and woman whom the old man in his cunning had spared.

Michael was soon to discover what was going to happen. The old man opened the door of the buffet and took out a great steel hook, at the end of which was a pulley. Reaching up, he slipped the end of the hook into a steel bolt, fastened in one of the overhead beams. Michael had noticed it before and wondered what purpose it served. He was now to learn.

From the cupboard came a long coil of rope, one end of which was threaded through the pulley and fastened dexterously under the detective's armpits. Stooping, Longvale lifted the carpet and rolled it up, and then Michael saw that there was a small trap-door, which he raised and laid back. Below he could see nothing, but there came to him the sound of a man's groaning.

"Now I think we can dispense with that, sir," said Mr Longvale, and untied the serviette that covered the detective's mouth.

This done, he pulled on the rope, seemingly without an effort, and Michael swung in mid-air. It was uncomfortable; he had an absurd notion that he looked a little ridiculous. The old man guided his feet through the opening and gradually paid out the rope.

"Will you be good enough to tell me when you touch ground," he asked, "and I will come down to you?"

Looking up, Michael saw the square in the floor grow smaller and smaller, and for an unconscionable time he swung and swayed and turned in mid-air. He thought he was not moving, and then, without warning, his feet touched ground and he called out.

"Are you all right?" said Mr Longvale pleasantly. "Do you mind stepping a few paces on one side? I am dropping the rope, and it may hurt you."

Michael gasped, but carried out instructions, and presently he heard the swish of the falling line and the smack of it as it struck the ground. Then the trap-door closed, and there was no other sound but the groaning near at hand.

"Is that you, Penne?"

"Who is it?" asked the other in a frightened voice. "Is it you, Brixan? Where are we? What has happened? How did I get here? That old devil gave me a drink. I ran out – and that's all I remember. I went to borrow his car. My God, I'm scared! The magneto of mine went wrong."

"Did you shout when you ran from the house?"

"I think I did. I felt this infernal poison taking effect and dashed out – I don't remember. Where are you, Brixan? The police will get us out of this, won't they?"

"Alive, I hope," said Michael grimly, and he heard the man's frightened sob, and was sorry he had spoken.

"What is he? Who is he? Are these the caves? I've heard about them. It smells horribly earthy, doesn't it? Can you see anything?"

"I thought I saw a light just then," said Michael, "but my eyes are playing tricks." And then: "Where is Adele Leamington?"

"God knows," said the other. He was shivering, and Michael heard the sound of his chattering teeth. "I never saw her again. I was afraid Bhag would go after her. But he wouldn't hurt her — he is a queer devil. I wish he was here now."

"I wish somebody was here," said Michael sincerely.

He was trying to work his wrists loose of the handcuffs, though he knew that barehanded he stood very little chance against the old man. He had lost his pistol, and although, in the inside of his waistcoat, there remained intact the long, razor-sharp knife that had cleared him out of many a Continental scrape, the one infallible weapon when firearms failed, he knew that he would have no opportunity for its employment.

Sitting down, he tried to perform a trick that he had seen on a stage in Berlin — the trick of bringing his legs through his manacled hands and so getting his hands in front of him, but he struggled without avail. There came the sound of a door opening, and Mr Longvale's voice.

"I won't keep you a moment," he said. He carried a lantern in his hand that swung as he walked, and seemed to intensify the gloom.

"I don't like my patients to catch cold."

His laughter came echoing back from the vaulted roof of the cave, intensified hideously. Stopping, he struck a match and a brilliant light appeared. It was a vapour lamp fixed on a shelf of rock. Presently he lit another, and then a third and a fourth, and, in the white, unwinking light, every object in the cave stood out with startling distinctness. Michael saw the scarlet thing that stood in the cave's centre, and, hardened as he was, and prepared for that fearsome sight, he shuddered.

It was a guillotine!

"THE WIDOW"

A GUILLOTINE!

Standing in the middle of the cave, its high framework lifted starkly. It was painted blood-red, and its very simplicity had a horror of its own.

Michael looked, fascinated. The basket, the bright, triangular knife suspended at the top of the frame, the tilted platform with its dangling straps, the black-painted lunette shaped to receive the head of the victim and hold it in position till the knife fell in its oiled groove. He knew the machine bolt by bolt, had seen it in operation on grey mornings before French prisons, with soldiers holding back the crowd, and a little group of officials in the centre of the cleared space. He knew the sound of it, the "*clop!*" as it fell, sweeping to eternity the man beneath.

" 'The Widow'!" said Longvale humorously. He touched the frame lovingly.

"Oh God, I'm not fit to die!" It was Penne's agonized wail that went echoing through the hollow spaces of the cavern.

"The Widow," murmured the old man again.

He was without a hat; his bald head shone in the light, yet there was nothing ludicrous in his appearance. His attitude toward this thing he loved was in a sense pathetic.

"Who shall be her first bridegroom?"

"Not me, not me!" squealed Penne, wriggling back against the wall, his face ashen, his mouth working convulsively. "I'm not fit to die – "

201

Longvale walked slowly over to him, stooped and raised him to his feet.

"Courage!" he murmured. "It is the hour!"

Jack Knebworth was pacing the road when the police car came flying back from Chichester.

"He's not there, hasn't been to the station at all," said the driver breathlessly as he flung out of the car.

"He may have gone into Longvale's house."

"I've seen Mr Longvale: it was he who told me that the Captain had gone into Chichester. He must have made a mistake."

Knebworth's jaw dropped. A great light suddenly flashed upon his mind. Longvale! There was something queer about him. Was it possible – ?

He remembered now that he had been puzzled by a contradictory statement the old man had made; remembered that, not once but many times, Sampson Longvale had expressed a desire to be filmed in a favourite part of his own, one that he had presented, an episode in the life of his famous ancestor.

"We'll go and knock him up. I'll talk to him."

They hammered at the door without eliciting a response.

"That's his bedroom." Jack Knebworth pointed to a latticed window where a light shone, and Inspector Lyle threw up a pebble with such violence that the glass was broken. Still there was no response.

"I don't like that," said Knebworth suddenly.

"You don't like it any better than I do," growled the officer. "Try that window, Smith."

"Do you want me to open it, sir?"

"Yes, without delay."

A second later, the window of the long dining-room was prized open; and then they came upon an obstacle which could not be so readily forced.

"The shutter is steel-lined," reported the detective. "I think I'd better try one of the upper rooms. Give me a leg up, somebody."

With the assistance of a fellow, he reached up and caught the sill of an open window, the very window from which Adele had looked down into the grinning face of Bhag. In another second he was in the room, and was reaching down to help up a second officer. A few minutes' delay, and the front door was unbarred and opened.

"There's nobody in the house, so far as I can find out," said the officer.

"Put a light on," ordered the inspector shortly.

They found the little vapour lamp and lit it.

"What's that?" The detective officer pointed to the hook that still hung in the beam with the pulley beneath, and his eyes narrowed. "I can't understand that," he said slowly. "What was that for?"

Jack Knebworth uttered an exclamation.

"Here's Brixan's gun!" he said, and picked it up from the floor.

One glance the inspector gave, and then his eyes went back to the hook and the pulley.

"That beats me," he said. "See if you fellows can find anything anywhere. Open every cupboard, every drawer. Sound the walls — there may be secret doors; there are in all these old Tudor houses."

The search was futile, and Inspector Lyle came back to a worried contemplation of the hook and pulley. Then one of his men came in to say that he had located the garage.

It was an unusually long building, and when it was opened, it revealed no more than the old-fashioned car which was a familiar object in that part of the country. But obviously, this was only half the accommodation. The seemingly solid whitewashed wall behind the machine hid another apartment, though it had no door, and an inspection of the outside showed a solid wall at the far end of the garage.

Jack Knebworth tapped the interior wall.

"This isn't brickwork at all, it's wood," he said.

Hanging in a corner was a chain. Apparently it had no particular function, but a careful scrutiny led to the discovery that the links ran through a hole in the roughly plastered ceiling. The inspector caught the chain and pulled, and, as he did so, the "wall" opened inwards, showing the contents of the second chamber, which was a second car, so sheeted that only its radiator was visible. Knebworth pulled off the cover, and: "That's the car."

"What car?" asked the inspector.

"The car driven by the Head-Hunter," said Knebworth quickly. "He was in that machine when Brixan tried to arrest him. I'd know it anywhere! Brixan is in the Dower House somewhere, and if he's in the hands of the Head-Hunter, God help him!"

They ran back to the house, and again the hook and pulley drew them as a magnet. Suddenly the police officer bent down and jerked back the carpet. The trap-door beneath the pulley was plainly visible. Pulling it open, he knelt down and gazed through. Knebworth saw his face grow haggard.

"Too late, too late!" he muttered.

THE DEATH

The shriek of a man half crazy with fear is not nice to hear. Michael's nerves were tough, but he had need to drive the nails into the palms of his manacled hands to keep his self-control.

"I warn you," he found voice to say, as the shrieking died to an unintelligible babble of sound, "Longvale, if you do this, you are everlastingly damned!"

The old man turned his quiet smile upon his second prisoner, but did not make any answer. Lifting the half-conscious man in his arms as easily as though he were a child, he carried him to the terrible machine, and laid him, face downwards, on the tilted platform. There was no hurry. Michael saw, in Longvale's leisure, an enjoyment that was unbelievable. He stepped to the front of the machine and pulled up one half of the lunette; there was a click, and it remained stationary.

"An invention of mine," he said with pride, speaking over his shoulder.

Michael looked away for a second, past the grim executioner, to the farther end of the cave. And then he saw a sight that brought the blood to his cheeks. At first he thought he was dreaming, and that the strain of his ordeal was responsible for some grotesque vision.

Adele!

She stood clear in the white light, so grimed with earth and dust that she seemed to be wearing a grey robe.

"If you move I will kill you!"

It was she! He twisted over on to his knees and staggered upright. Longvale heard the voice and turned slowly.

"My little lady," he said pleasantly. "How providential! I've always thought that the culminating point of my career would be, as was the sainted Charles Henry's, that moment when a queen came under his hand. How very singular!"

He walked slowly toward her, oblivious to the pointed pistol, to the danger in which he stood, a radiant smile on his face, his small, white hands extended as to an honoured guest.

"Shoot!" cried Michael hoarsely. "For God's sake, shoot!"

She hesitated for a second and pressed the trigger. There was no sound – clogged with earth, the delicate mechanism did not act.

She turned to flee, but his arm was round her, and his disengaged hand drew her head to his breast.

"You shall see, my dear," he said. "The Widow shall become the Widower, and you shall be his first bride!"

She was limp in his arms now, incapable of resistance. A strange sense of inertia overcame her; and, though she was conscious, she could neither of her own volition, move nor speak. Michael, struggling madly to release his hands, prayed that she might faint – that, whatever happened, she should be spared a consciousness of the terror.

"Now who shall be first?" murmured the old man, stroking his shiny head. "It would be fitting that my lady should show the way, and be spared the agony of mind. And yet – " He looked thoughtfully at the prostrate figure strapped to the board, and, tilting the platform, dropped the lunette about the head of Gregory Penne. The hand went up to the lever that controlled the knife. He paused again, evidently puzzling something out in his crazy mind.

"No, you shall be first," he said, unbuckled the strap and pushed the half-demented man to the ground.

Michael saw him lift his head, listening. There were hollow sounds above, as of people walking. Again he changed his mind, stooped and dragged Gregory Penne to his feet. Michael wondered why he held him so long, standing so rigidly; wondered why he dropped him suddenly to the ground; and then wondered no longer. Something was crossing the floor of the cave – a great, hairy something, whose malignant eyes were turned upon the old man.

It was Bhag! His hair was matted with blood; his face wore the powder mask which Michael had seen when he emerged from Griff Towers. He stopped and sniffed at the groaning man on the floor, and his big paw touched the face tenderly. Then, without preliminary, he leapt at Longvale, and the old man went down with a crash to the ground, his arms whirling in futile defence. For a second Bhag stood over him, looking down, twittering and chattering; and then he raised the man and laid him in the place where his master had been, tilting the board and pushing it forward.

Michael gazed with fascinated horror. The great ape had witnessed an execution! It was from this cave that he had escaped, the night that Foss was killed. His half-human mind was remembering the details. Michael could almost see his mind working to recall the procedure.

Bhag fumbled with the frame, touched the spring that released the lunette, and it fell over the neck of the Head-Hunter. And at that moment, attracted by a sound, Michael looked up, saw the trap above pulled back. Bhag heard it also, but was too intent upon his business to be interrupted. Longvale had recovered consciousness and was fighting to draw his head from the lunette. Presently he spoke. It was as though he realized the imminence of his fate, and was struggling to find an appropriate phrase, for he lay quiescent now, his hands gripping the edge of the narrow platform on which he lay.

"Son of St Louis, ascend to heaven!" he said, and at that moment Bhag jerked the handle that controlled the knife.

Inspector Lyle from above saw the blade fall, heard the indescribable sound of the thud that followed, and almost swooned. Then, from below: "It's all right, inspector. You may find a rope in the buffet. Get down as quickly as you can and bring a gun."

The buffet cupboard contained another rope, and a minute later the detective was going down hand over hand.

"There's no danger from the monkey," said Michael.

Bhag was crooning over his senseless master, as a mother over her child.

"Get Miss Leamington away," said Michael in a low voice, as the detective began to unlock the handcuffs.

The girl lay, an inanimate and silent figure, by the side of the guillotine, happily oblivious of the tragedy which had been enacted in her presence. Another detective had descended the rope, and old Jack Knebworth, despite his years, was the third to enter the cave. It was he who found the door, and aided the detective to carry the girl to safety.

Unlocking the handcuffs from the baronet's wrists, Michael turned him over on his back. One glance at the face told the detective that the man was in a fit, and that his case, if not hopeless, was at least desperate. As though understanding that the man had no ill intent toward his master, Bhag watched passively, and then Michael remembered how, the first time he had seen the great ape, Bhag had smelt his hands.

"He's filing you for future reference as a friend," had said Gregory at the time.

"Pick him up," said Michael, speaking distinctly in the manner that Gregory had addressed the ape.

Without hesitation, Bhag stooped and lifted the limp man in his arms, and Michael guided him to the stairway and led him up the stairs.

The house was full of police, who gaped at the sight of the great ape and his burden.

"Take him upstairs and put him on the bed," ordered Michael.

Knebworth had already taken the girl off in his car to Chichester, for she had shown signs of reviving, and he wanted to get her away from that house of the dead before she fully recovered.

Michael went down into the cave again and joined the inspector. Together they made a brief tour. The headless figures in the niches told their own story. Farther on, Michael came to the bigger cavern, with its floor littered with bones.

"Here is confirmation of the old legend," he said in a hushed voice, and pointed. "These are the bones of those warriors and squires who were trapped in the cave by a landslide. You can see the horses' skeletons quite plainly."

How had Adele got into the cave? He was not long before he found the slide down which she had tumbled.

"Another mystery is explained," he said. "Griff Tower was obviously built by the Romans to prevent cattle and men from falling through into the cave. Incidentally, it has served as an excellent ventilator, and I have no doubt the old man had this way prepared, both as a hiding place for the people he had killed and as a way of escape."

He saw a candle-lantern and matches that the girl had missed, and this he regarded as conclusive proof that his view was right.

They came back to the guillotine with its ghastly burden, and Michael stood in silence for a long time, looking at the still figure stretched on the platform, its hands still clutching the sides.

"How did he persuade these people to come to their death?" asked the inspector in a voice little above a whisper.

"That is a question for the psychologist," said Michael at last. "There is no doubt that he got into touch with many men who were contemplating suicide but shrank from the act, and performed this service for them. I should imagine his practice of leaving around their heads for identification arose out of some poor wretch's desire that his wife and family should secure his insurance.

"He worked with extraordinary cunning. The letters, as you know, went to a house of call and were collected by an old woman, who posted them to a second address, whence they were put in prepared envelopes and posted, ostensibly to London. I discovered that the envelopes were kept in a specially light-proof box, and that the unknown advertiser had stipulated that they should not be taken out of that box until they were ready for posting. An hour after those letters were put in the mail the address faded and became invisible, and another appeared."

"Vanishing ink?"

Mike nodded.

"It is a trick that criminals frequently employ. The new address, of course, was Dower House. Put out the lights and let us go up."

Three lamps were extinguished, and the detective looked round fearfully at the shadows.

"I think we'll leave this down here," he said.

"I think we will," said Michael, in complete agreement.

CAMERA!

Three months had passed since the Dower House had yielded up its grisly secrets. A long enough time for Gregory Penne to recover completely and to have served one of the six months' imprisonment to which he was sentenced on a technical charge. The guillotine had been re-erected in a certain Black Museum on the Thames Embankment, where young policemen come to look upon the equipment of criminality. People had ceased to talk about the Head-Hunter.

It seemed a million years ago to Michael as he sat, perched on a table, watching Jack Knebworth, in the last stages of despair, directing a ruffled Reggie Connolly in the business of love-making. Near by stood Adele Leamington, a star by virtue of the success that had attended a certain trade show.

Out of range of the camera, a cigarette between her fingers, Stella Mendoza, gorgeously attired, watched her some time friend and prospective leading man with good-natured contempt.

"There's nobody can tell me, Mr Knebworth," said Reggie testily, "how to hold a girl! Good gracious, heavens alive, have I been asleep all my life? Don't you think I know as much about girls as you, Mr Knebworth?"

"I don't care a darn how you hold your girl," howled Jack. "I'm telling you how to hold *my* girl! There's only one way of making love, and that's *my* way. I've got the patent rights! Your arm round her waist again, Connolly. Hold your head up, will you? Now turn it this way. Now drop your chin a little. Smile, darn you, smile! Not a prop smile!" he shrieked. "Smile as if you liked her. Try to imagine that she loves you! I'll apologize to you, afterwards, Adele, but try to imagine it, Connolly. That's better. You look as if you'd swallowed a liqueur of broken glass! Look down into her eyes – look, I said, not glare! That's better. Now do that again – "

He watched, writhing, gesticulating, and at last, in cold resignation: "Rotten, but it'll have to do. Lights!"

The big Kreisler lights flared, the banked mercury lamps burnt bluely, and the flood lamps became blank expanses of diffused light. Again the rehearsal went through, and then: "Camera!" wailed Jack, and the handle began to turn.

"That's all for you today, Connolly," said Jack. "Now, Miss Mendoz – "

Adele came across to where Michael was sitting and jumped up on to the table beside him.

"Mr Knebworth is quite right," she said, shaking her head. "Reggie Connolly doesn't know how to make love."

"Who does?" demanded Michael. "Except the right man?"

"He's supposed to be the right man," she insisted. "And, what's more, he's supposed to be the best lover on the English screen."

"Ha ha!" said Michael sardonically.

She was silent for a time, and then: "Why are you still here? I thought your work was finished in this part of the world."

"Not all," he said cheerfully. "I've still an arrest to make."

She looked up at him quickly.

"Another?" she said. "I thought, when you took poor Sir Gregory – "

"Poor Sir Gregory!" he scoffed. "He ought to be a very happy man. Six months' hard labour was just what he wanted, and he was lucky to be charged, not with the killing of his unfortunate servant but with the concealment of his death."

"Whom are you arresting now?"

"I'm not so sure," said Michael, "whether I shall arrest her."

"Is it a woman?"

He nodded.

"What has she done?"

"The charge isn't definitely settled," he said evasively, "but I think there will be several counts. Creating a disturbance will be one; deliberately endangering public health – at any rate, the health of one of the public – will be another; maliciously wounding the feelings – "

"Oh, *you*, you mean?"

She laughed softly.

"I thought that was part of your delirium that night at the hospital, or part of mine. But as other people saw you kiss me, it must have been yours. I don't think I want to marry," she said thoughtfully. "I am – "

"Don't say that you are wedded to your art," he groaned. "They all say that!"

"No, I'm not wedded to anything, except a desire to prevent my best friend from making a great mistake. You've a very big career in front of you, Michael, and marrying me is not going to help you. People will think you're just infatuated, and when the inevitable divorce comes along – "

They both laughed together.

"If you have finished being like a maiden aunt, I want to tell you something," said Michael. "I've loved you from the moment I saw you."

"Of course you have," she said calmly. "That's the only possible way you *can* love a girl. If it takes three days to make up your mind it can't be love. That's why I know I don't love you. I was annoyed with you the first time I met you; I was furious with you the second time; and I've just tolerated you ever since. Wait till I get my make-up off."

She got down and ran to her dressing-room. Michael strolled across to comfort an exhausted Jack Knebworth.

"Adele? Oh, she's all right. She really has had an offer from America – not Hollywood, but a studio in the East. I've advised her not to take it until she's a little more proficient, but I don't think she wanted any advice. That girl isn't going to stay in the picture business."

"What makes you think that, Knebworth?"

"She's going to get married," said Jack glumly. "I can recognize the signs. I told you all along that there was something queer about her. She's going to get married and leave the screen for good – that's her eccentricity."

"And whom do you think she will marry?" asked Michael.

Old Jack snorted.

"It won't be Reggie Connolly – that I can promise you."

"I should jolly well say not!" said that indignant young man, who had remarkably keen ears. "I'm not a marrying chap. It spoils an artist. A wife is like a millstone round his neck. He has no chance of expressing his individuality. And whilst we are on that subject, Mr Knebworth, are you perfectly sure that I'm to blame? Doesn't it strike you – mind you, I wouldn't say a word against the dear girl – doesn't it strike you that Miss Leamington isn't quite – what shall I say? – seasoned in love – that's the expression."

Stella Mendoza had strolled up. She had returned to the scene of her former labours, and it looked very much as if she were coming back to her former position.

"When you say 'seasoned' you mean 'smoked,' Reggie," she said. "I think you're wrong."

"I can't be wrong," said Reggie complacently. "I've made love to more girls in this country than any other five leading men, and I tell you that Miss Leamington is distinctly and fearfully immature."

The object of their discussion appeared at the end of the studio, nodded a cheery good night to the company and went out, Michael on her heels.

"You're fearfully immature," he said, as he guided her across the road.

"Who said so? It sounds like Reggie: that is a favourite word of his."

"He says you know nothing whatever about love-making."

"Perhaps I don't," she said shortly, and so baffling was her tone that he was not prepared to continue the subject, until they reached the long, dark road in which she lived.

"The proper way to make love," he said, more than a little appalled at his own boldness, "is to put one hand on the waist – "

Suddenly she was in his arms, her cool face against his.

"There isn't any way," she murmured. "One just does!"

Edgar Wallace

Big Foot

Footprints and a dead woman bring together Superintendent Minton and the amateur sleuth Mr Cardew. Who is the man in the shrubbery? Who is the singer of the haunting Moorish tune? Why is Hannah Shaw so determined to go to Pawsy, 'a dog lonely place' she had previously detested? Death lurks in the dark and someone must solve the mystery before BIG FOOT strikes again, in a yet more fiendish manner.

Bones In London

The new Managing Director of Schemes Ltd has an elegant London office and a theatrically dressed assistant – however Bones, as he is better known, is bored. Luckily there is a slump in the shipping market and it is not long before Joe and Fred Pole pay Bones a visit. They are totally unprepared for Bones' unnerving style of doing business, unprepared for his unique style of innocent and endearing mischief.

EDGAR WALLACE

BONES OF THE RIVER

'Taking the little paper from the pigeon's leg, Hamilton saw it was from Sanders and marked URGENT. *Send Bones instantly to Lujamalababa… Arrest and bring to head-quarters the witch doctor.*'

It is a time when the world's most powerful nations are vying for colonial honour, a time of trading steamers and tribal chiefs. In the mysterious African territories administered by Commissioner Sanders, Bones persistently manages to create his own unique style of innocent and endearing mischief.

THE DAFFODIL MYSTERY

When Mr Thomas Lyne, poet, poseur and owner of Lyne's Emporium insults a cashier, Odette Rider, she resigns. Having summoned detective Jack Tarling to investigate another employee, Mr Milburgh, Lyne now changes his plans. Tarling and his Chinese companion refuse to become involved. They pay a visit to Odette's flat. In the hall Tarling meets Sam, convicted felon and protégé of Lyne. Next morning Tarling discovers a body. The hands are crossed on the breast, adorned with a handful of daffodils.

Edgar Wallace

The Joker

While the millionaire Stratford Harlow is in Princetown, not only does he meet with his lawyer Mr Ellenbury but he gets his first glimpse of the beautiful Aileen Rivers, niece of the actor and convicted felon Arthur Ingle. When Aileen is involved in a car accident on the Thames Embankment, the driver is James Carlton of Scotland Yard. Later that evening Carlton gets a call. It is Aileen. She needs help.

The Square Emerald

'Suicide on the left,' says Chief Inspector Coldwell pleasantly, as he and Leslie Maughan stride along the Thames Embankment during a brutally cold night. A gaunt figure is sprawled across the parapet. But Coldwell soon discovers that Peter Dawlish, fresh out of prison for forgery, is not considering suicide but murder. Coldwell suspects Druze as the intended victim. Maughan disagrees. If Druze dies, she says, 'It will be because he does not love children!'

OTHER TITLES BY EDGAR WALLACE AVAILABLE DIRECT
FROM HOUSE OF STRATUS

Quantity		£	$(US)	$(CAN)	€
	THE ADMIRABLE CARFEW	6.99	11.50	15.99	11.50
	THE ANGEL OF TERROR	6.99	11.50	15.99	11.50
	BARBARA ON HER OWN	6.99	11.50	15.99	11.50
	BIG FOOT	6.99	11.50	15.99	11.50
	THE BLACK ABBOT	6.99	11.50	15.99	11.50
	BONES	6.99	11.50	15.99	11.50
	BONES IN LONDON	6.99	11.50	15.99	11.50
	BONES OF THE RIVER	6.99	11.50	15.99	11.50
	THE CLUE OF THE NEW PIN	6.99	11.50	15.99	11.50
	THE CLUE OF THE SILVER KEY	6.99	11.50	15.99	11.50
	THE CLUE OF THE TWISTED CANDLE	6.99	11.50	15.99	11.50
	THE COAT OF ARMS	6.99	11.50	15.99	11.50
	THE COUNCIL OF JUSTICE	6.99	11.50	15.99	11.50
	THE CRIMSON CIRCLE	6.99	11.50	15.99	11.50
	THE DAFFODIL MYSTERY	6.99	11.50	15.99	11.50
	THE DARK EYES OF LONDON	6.99	11.50	15.99	11.50
	THE DAUGHTERS OF THE NIGHT	6.99	11.50	15.99	11.50
	A DEBT DISCHARGED	6.99	11.50	15.99	11.50
	THE DEVIL MAN	6.99	11.50	15.99	11.50
	THE DOOR WITH SEVEN LOCKS	6.99	11.50	15.99	11.50
	THE DUKE IN THE SUBURBS	6.99	11.50	15.99	11.50
	THE FACE IN THE NIGHT	6.99	11.50	15.99	11.50
	THE FEATHERED SERPENT	6.99	11.50	15.99	11.50
	THE FLYING SQUAD	6.99	11.50	15.99	11.50
	THE FORGER	6.99	11.50	15.99	11.50
	THE FOUR JUST MEN	6.99	11.50	15.99	11.50
	FOUR SQUARE JANE	6.99	11.50	15.99	11.50

ALL HOUSE OF STRATUS BOOKS ARE AVAILABLE FROM GOOD BOOKSHOPS
OR DIRECT FROM THE PUBLISHER:

Internet: **www.houseofstratus.com** including author interviews, reviews, features.

Email: **sales@houseofstratus.com** please quote author, title and credit card details.

OTHER TITLES BY EDGAR WALLACE AVAILABLE DIRECT
FROM HOUSE OF STRATUS

Quantity		£	$(US)	$(CAN)	€
	THE FOURTH PLAGUE	6.99	11.50	15.99	11.50
	THE FRIGHTENED LADY	6.99	11.50	15.99	11.50
	GOOD EVANS	6.99	11.50	15.99	11.50
	THE HAND OF POWER	6.99	11.50	15.99	11.50
	THE IRON GRIP	6.99	11.50	15.99	11.50
	THE JOKER	6.99	11.50	15.99	11.50
	THE JUST MEN OF CORDOVA	6.99	11.50	15.99	11.50
	THE KEEPERS OF THE KING'S PEACE	6.99	11.50	15.99	11.50
	THE LAW OF THE FOUR JUST MEN	6.99	11.50	15.99	11.50
	THE LONE HOUSE MYSTERY	6.99	11.50	15.99	11.50
	THE MAN WHO BOUGHT LONDON	6.99	11.50	15.99	11.50
	THE MAN WHO KNEW	6.99	11.50	15.99	11.50
	THE MAN WHO WAS NOBODY	6.99	11.50	15.99	11.50
	THE MIND OF MR J G REEDER	6.99	11.50	15.99	11.50
	MORE EDUCATED EVANS	6.99	11.50	15.99	11.50
	MR J G REEDER RETURNS	6.99	11.50	15.99	11.50
	MR JUSTICE MAXELL	6.99	11.50	15.99	11.50
	RED ACES	6.99	11.50	15.99	11.50
	ROOM 13	6.99	11.50	15.99	11.50
	SANDERS	6.99	11.50	15.99	11.50
	SANDERS OF THE RIVER	6.99	11.50	15.99	11.50
	THE SINISTER MAN	6.99	11.50	15.99	11.50
	THE SQUARE EMERALD	6.99	11.50	15.99	11.50
	THE THREE JUST MEN	6.99	11.50	15.99	11.50
	THE THREE OAK MYSTERY	6.99	11.50	15.99	11.50
	THE TRAITOR'S GATE	6.99	11.50	15.99	11.50
	WHEN THE GANGS CAME TO LONDON	6.99	11.50	15.99	11.50

Hotline: UK ONLY: 0800 169 1780, please quote author, title and credit card details.
INTERNATIONAL: +44 (0) 20 7494 6400, please quote author, title and credit card details.

Send to: House of Stratus Sales Department
24c Old Burlington Street
London
W1X 1RL
UK

Please allow for postage costs charged per order plus an amount per book as set out in the tables below:

	£(Sterling)	$(US)	$(CAN)	€(Euros)
Cost per order				
UK	1.50	2.25	3.50	2.50
Europe	3.00	4.50	6.75	5.00
North America	3.00	4.50	6.75	5.00
Rest of World	3.00	4.50	6.75	5.00
Additional cost per book				
UK	0.50	0.75	1.15	0.85
Europe	1.00	1.50	2.30	1.70
North America	2.00	3.00	4.60	3.40
Rest of World	2.50	3.75	5.75	4.25

PLEASE SEND CHEQUE, POSTAL ORDER (STERLING ONLY), EUROCHEQUE, OR INTERNATIONAL MONEY ORDER (PLEASE CIRCLE METHOD OF PAYMENT YOU WISH TO USE)
MAKE PAYABLE TO: STRATUS HOLDINGS plc

Cost of book(s): —————— Example: 3 x books at £6.99 each: £20.97

Cost of order: —————— Example: £2.00 (Delivery to UK address)

Additional cost per book: —————— Example: 3 x £0.50: £1.50

Order total including postage: —————— Example: £24.47

Please tick currency you wish to use and add total amount of order:

☐ £ (Sterling)   ☐ $ (US)   ☐ $ (CAN)   ☐ € (EUROS)

VISA, MASTERCARD, SWITCH, AMEX, SOLO, JCB:

☐ ☐ ☐ ☐ ☐ ☐ ☐ ☐ ☐ ☐ ☐ ☐ ☐ ☐ ☐ ☐ ☐ ☐

Issue number (Switch only):

☐ ☐ ☐

Start Date:

☐ ☐ / ☐ ☐

Expiry Date:

☐ ☐ / ☐ ☐

Signature: ————————————

NAME: ————————————

ADDRESS: ————————————

————————————

POSTCODE: ————————

Please allow 28 days for delivery.

Prices subject to change without notice.
Please tick box if you do not wish to receive any additional information. ☐

House of Stratus publishes many other titles in this genre; please check our website (**www.houseofstratus.com**) for more details.